WESTERN

TH

THE TRAIL OF THE APACHE KID

Lewis B. Patten

Chivers Press
Bath, England

G.K. Hall & Co.
Thorndike, Maine USA

This Large Print edition is published by Chivers Press, England, and by G.K. Hall & Co., USA.

Published in 1998 in the U.K. by arrangement with Golden West Literary Agency.

Published in 1998 in the U.S. by arrangement with Golden West Literary Agency.

U.K. Hardcover ISBN 0–7540–3431–3 (Chivers Large Print)
U.K. Softcover ISBN 0–7540–3432–1 (Camden Large Print)
U.S. Softcover ISBN 0–7838–0245–5 (Nightingale Series Edition)

The text of this Large Print edition is unabridged.
Other aspects of the book may vary from the original edition.

Set in 16 pt. New Times Roman.

Printed in Great Britain on acid-free paper.

British Library Cataloguing in Publication Data available

Library of Congress Cataloging-in-Publication Data

Patten, Lewis B.
The trail of the Apache Kid / Lewis B. Patten.
p. cm.
ISBN 0–7838–0245–5 (lg. print : sc. : alk. paper)
1. Large type books. I. Title.
[PS3566.A79T73 1998]
813'.54—dc21 98–21235

CHAPTER ONE

He came riding down the long slope out of the grassy hills to the north in early evening after a day of greasing and repairing windmills. Tall and browned by a lifetime of exposure to sun and wind, he sat loose and relaxed in his saddle, looking forward to the supper he knew his wife Nora and María Martínez would have ready for him as soon as he had put away his horses and washed.

Frank Healy was a hard-muscled, rawboned man, dressed in a faded pair of blue Army sergeant's trousers with darker blue stripes down the sides showing where the yellow stripes had been, and a blue Army shirt. His broad-brimmed hat was stained with sweat and dust at the base of the crown. His boots were run-over at the heels and badly scuffed.

The cluster of ranch buildings became visible to him when he topped a knoll half a mile away and he felt his breath sigh slowly out. He puzzled over that, realizing he had experienced distinct relief just at seeing the buildings there intact.

What the hell had he expected anyway? Yet in spite of himself, a strange, uncomfortable feeling of uneasiness stayed with him and because it did he touched spurs to his horse's sides. The animal broke into a trot. Behind, the packhorse kept pace, the panniers loaded with wire, tools and grease banging against his sides.

Healy could see chickens in the yard. But no smoke from the chimney. And the two horses he'd left in the corral were gone.

Suddenly his uneasiness became very strong. He spurred his horse again, forcing the animal to lope. The packhorse lagged, so Healy took a turn around the saddle horn with the halter rope.

He kept telling himself that he was imagining things. There would be an explanation forthcoming for the horses that were missing from the corral and for the fact that no smoke came from the chimney even though it was suppertime.

From a quarter mile it seemed to take forever to reach the place. He rode into the yard, his feeling of uneasiness reaching the proportions of panic as he saw the dog, a tan mongrel named Duke, lying dead not a dozen feet from the back door. There was a spot of dried blood on the dog's side as big as Healy's hand.

Healy hit the ground running and burst through the kitchen door, only to stop immediately. Fear turned his chest to ice. Two bodies lay in the middle of the kitchen floor, María Martínez and her husband Francisco. Both their throats had been cut. There was blood on everything, as if someone had been killing chickens here. Apparently Francisco had not stopped fighting even after his throat was cut.

Frank Healy's voice came out in a tortured roar. 'Nora! Nora! For God's sake, are you all right?'

Only silence answered him. He stood there, still a moment, and then silently drew his gun. He thumbed the hammer back. He knew he ought to move into this with care and he tried to restrain himself but failed. With an agonized sound of pain, he leaped over the bodies of Francisco and María and charged into the main part of the house like a maddened bull.

Nothing in the parlor; nothing in the downstairs bedroom; nothing in any of the closets. He took the stairs three at a time and searched the upstairs bedrooms similarly. There was no sign of his wife, no sign of the marauder, no sign, even, of violence. Frank Healy ran back down the stairs and out into the dying light of day.

The sun was below the rounded hills to the west, but its rays stained the clouds a brilliant orange. By this light, Healy quested like a hound, across the yard and beyond.

He found, first, the small footprints of Nora, scuffed as if she was being forced. Beside these he found the unmistakable prints of an Apache's moccasins.

He followed them to the corral. Two bridles were gone from the nails where they customarily hung. Otherwise, it was only the tracks, the tracks of the two horses crossing the yard at a lope and heading west.

Healy felt sick at his stomach. His chest felt so empty it ached. Questing still and wanting to be sure, he crossed the yard to its western edge and then made a large semicircle, his eyes fixed steadily on the ground. He found the moccasin tracks again; the Indian had watched the house for quite some time. Following the moccasin tracks back the way they had come, he came upon a short-legged, shaggy horse, dead, his throat cut too.

Slowly he walked back and stopped at last, in the middle of the yard, not ten feet from the body of the mongrel Duke. And now he knew for sure. He recognized the work of this Indian. Somehow, someway, the Apache Kid had escaped from prison in Florida. Or he'd been released. He'd come here—God only knew how he'd found the place—to exact revenge against Frank Healy, whom he blamed for his capture and incarceration in Florida for the past two years.

Before his marriage to Nora, Healy had scouted for the Army, operating out of Fort Chiricahua, a hundred and seventy-five miles west of here, and he could still track like an Apache. He hadn't forgotten that in the two years since he had brought Nora Corcoran here to western New Mexico to ranch.

He knew the Kid's trail was six or seven hours old and he knew he couldn't follow it in the dark.

He also knew the Apache Kid would probably travel forty or fifty miles before he stopped. He himself would reach the Kid's first camp tomorrow and he'd probably find Nora there, ravaged, perhaps tortured, but almost certainly dead.

He fought bitterly against the pain that line of thinking brought, telling himself that if the Kid had meant to kill Nora immediately he'd have done it here. He wouldn't have bothered taking her along with him.

The Kid usually traveled with a randomly kidnapped Indian woman. He worked her, and used her, but when she could no longer keep up or do the work he assigned her, he killed her with neither warning nor feeling of any kind.

If this was to be Nora's role, then he had a chance, he told himself. He'd caught the Kid once before and he could catch him again. But could he catch him in time? Before Nora's strength gave out and the Kid cut her throat?

His whole body was cold and he was shaking violently. The sun was completely gone now, and dusk lay across the land.

He went to the barn and got a shovel. He walked out behind the house by about a hundred yards and began to dig.

Slowly, slowly the exertion steadied him. When his breath ran out, he stopped and leaned for a time against the side of the grave.

Nora was no weakling. She was strong and

competent. She knew the Apache Kid and the things of which he was capable by now as well as her third husband did. If she hadn't seen him kill Francisco and María, then she had, at least, seen the bodies and the bloody kitchen atferward. He'd had to drag her to the corral. But once mouted, and headed away from her home, she would accept the inevitable. She would come to terms with what had happened to her without getting hysterical. As long as her strenght held out, she'd do nothing foolish that woullld bring the wrath of the Kid down on her.

Rested, he began to dig again. The ground was hard. He had no intention of going down six feet. He only wanted a grave deep enough to protect the bodies. They could be reburied later after a proper service by a priest.

Frank Healy worked hard, in the exertion finding a measure of peace from his tortured thoughts. At last, near ten o' clock, he decided the single grave was deep enough.

He climbed out and went into the house. He got two blankets and wrapped Francisco's body in one, María's in the other. One after the other, he carried them out to the grave. He had dug it wide enough for them both so by getting down into it, he was able to lift their bodies in.

He climbed out. He was not Catholic himself, but knew both María and Francisco were. He hesitated, at a loss for the proper words to say. Finally he simply crossed himself.

the way he had seen them do and began to fill in the grave.

He didn't stop until it was done. He rested a few moments, then carefully mouded the remaining loose earth over the grave.

He crossed the yard to the dog. Nora had been very fond of Duke, and the dog had never failed to greet him with wagging tail when he came home. He picked up the dog's body and carried it behind the house. Quickly he dug a smaller grave about fifty feet from the one he'd dug for Francisco and María earlier. He buried the dog, then mounted his horse and rode southeast toward the fenced pasture where the rest of his horses were.

He dropped the wire gate and rode in. The horses heard him and approached the gate curiously. He circled and drove them through it and back to the house. They went willingly enough into the corral.

The night was now pitch black. Clouds had spread across the sky blocking out what little light would otherwise have come from the stars. Healy went to the house, got a lantern and lighted it. He carried it to the corral. He selected the two strongest horses, then turned the others out. He unsaddled his own horse and turned him in with the others, then got some oats, dumped a measure for each of the three horses into a wooden trough he had provided for that purpose. He carried several huge forks of hay from the barn and threw them into the corral.

The horse he had used for a packhorse today he unsaddled and turned loose. He dumped the panniers out in the barn, then put a large sack of oats into one of them. Into the other he put two canteens which he had rinsed and filled at the pump. Lastly, he got some provisions for himself from the kitchen and put them into an old flour sack. He put this sack in with the canteens.

Now, with nothing more to do, his thoughts returned to Nora in the hands of the Apache Kid. His face twisted with anguish because he couldn't know for sure what the Kid was going to do with her. And he wouldn't know until sometime late tomorrow afternoon when he reached the Kid's first camp. The thought that Nora might already be dead was like a knife. The thought that the Kid might even now be torturing her was unbearable.

He lay down on the bed without removing his clothes and stared into the blackness overhead. He closed his eyes but he couldn't go to sleep.

He told himself that he needed the sleep if he was to be clear-eyed and effective tomorrow. He closed his eyes again and determinedly kept them closed.

But all he saw was Nora, her face that never seemed to tan but which only burned and freckled despite her half Mexican heritage. In complexion she took after her father, Mike

heckout
heck us out on Facebook
nd Instagram!
40.349.5500
itle: Outlaw canyon [large print]
Due: 6/6/2023
itle: The trial at Apache Junction [large print]
Due: 6/6/2023
itle: Ride the red trail [large print] : western trio
Due: 6/6/2023
itle: The trail of the Apache Kid [large rint]
Due: 6/6/2023
CL DOWNTOWN NEWARK
40-349-5500
ollow us on
acebook and Instagram!

---

ickingcountylibrary.org

Corcoran, a career sergeant stationed at Fort Chiricahua until his death in a skirmish with Apaches a year ago. But her eyes were dark and so was her hair, both legacies from her Mexican mother, who had died when she was five.

Mike Corcoran raised her with the help of Maggie Gleason, a laundress at the fort. If raising it could be called. Frank Healy felt a grin touch his mouth as he remembered the leggy youngster, running and playing with the boys instead of with the girls, and fighting with them too with a ferocity that sometimes necessitated forcible separation of the two combatants. No, Healy thought, the Apache Kid wouldn't break Nora easily.

The grin disappeared, then reappeared as he remembered the way Mike Corcoran had despaired of ever making a lady out of her. He remembered Mike's rantings and ravings. And he remembered the time, too, when he'd looked at Nora himself and had seen that she was suddenly a woman and no longer a little girl.

Determinedly he put thought out of his head and counted patiently, trying to make himself relax enough to go to sleep. But pictures kept appearing before his mind. A picture of the Apache Kid, short, powerful, and a picture of the Kid's face and of his eyes. The Kid was maybe twenty-five years old, Healy guessed. His face was smooth and dark and he had yet to grow even the beginnings of a beard unless he plucked out the hairs as soon as they appeared. Like all the men of his tribe he wore his black hair cut shoulder length, with a band of cloth, usually red, tied around his forehead to keep it out of his eyes.

The eyes of all Apaches are dark, nearly to the point of being black. They are all inscrutable, at least to most white men. Healy had, of course, discovered that when you got to know an Apache, you found his eyes to be just as expressive as anybody else's. But the Kid was an exception to this rule. His eyes were two bits of polished obsidian. They showed you nothing, neither hate, nor anger, nor satisfaction, nor any other human emotion. They were simply eyes, for the purpose of seeing and nothing else.

The Apache Kid was, purely and simply, a killing machine. Healy didn't know to this day whether he got pleasure out of killing or not. He just killed everything and everybody that had no use to him. Horses, when he had worn them out. Dogs, if their barking annoyed him. But mostly people, preferably but not necessarily white. And that meant Nora, the first time she faltered. Even babies and children were not spared.

He should have killed the Kid himself, he thought, two years ago when he ran him down and wore him out and caught him with an empty gun. He should have killed him in the same unthinking, automatic way he would have killed a big coiled rattler. But he hadn't and now it was too late.

His thoughts ran on for a while after that, and he remembered little things that had happened at Fort Chiricahua, and other things that were very private between Nora and himself.

But at last he went to sleep. A deep sleep of exhaustion from which he did not awaken until the gray of dawn came creeping into the room.

He got up at once, wide awake, and hurried from the house. He saddled the horse he had been riding yesterday. He put the packsaddle on a second horse, then hung the panniers in place and lashed them down, knowing he would be traveling fast all day. He haltered the third horse and tied the halter rope to the tail of the pack animal.

He pried up a loose board in the bedroom and got out the tin box that contained all the money he and Nora had. He went out, closed the door, mounted and took the trail of the Apache Kid without looking back.

CHAPTER TWO

The land Healy had chosen for his ranch lay in a natural drainage far west of the rich Rio Grande valley. It was watered by a stream that had no name and was dry except in spring and sometimes in summer after a heavy rain. But he had ditched it and spread what water there was out across the natural hayfield below the house, and he managed to put up something in the neighborhood of fifty tons of hay a year which he used for his horses and, sometimes, to feed his cattle when the ground was deeply covered with snow.

The hills around the ranch were gently rounded and mostly grassed, but as he traveled westward, the land became more arid, the grass thinner and various varieties of cactus began to appear.

In daylight, the trail was easily followed, even at a steady lope. The Kid was traveling fast, alternating his pace between a dead run and a lope, and this, of course, was the reason the U. S. Army always had so much difficulty catching renegade individuals or small groups of Apache bucks off the reservation. The big cavalry remounts could not, in the first place, maintain the pace set by the short-legged horses the Apaches used, particularly in rough or rocky country, which meant most of Arizona Territory.

In the second place, the soldiers paced their mounts. It could be a court-martial offense to ride an Army horse to death no matter what the justification for it might be. The Apaches rode theirs to death as a matter of expediency, and when they had, cut meat from the dead animal and used it to keep themselves alive.

Having ridden their horses to death, they had only to continue on foot until they found a ranch or settlement where more horses could be stolen, and perhaps more white people killed.

Healy tried to maintain the same pace as had the Kid. Where the Kid forced his two horses into a run, Healy did likewise. If the Kid let his horses lope, so did Healy. The hours passed.

In late morning, Healy came to a place where the Kid had briefly stopped to let his horses drink from a trickle of water in a deep ravine. Healy listened to his own three horses trying to suck up a satisfactory drink from the shallow, narrow flow, and studied the tracks made by the Kid and by Nora. The Kid and Nora had stayed here, he guessed, no more than ten minutes. Hardly enough time for the horses' breathing to return to normal. Certainly not enough time for them to rest.

He dragged his horses away from the water by force. He mounted and spurred the horse he was riding and all three lunged up the far side of the ravine.

Healy knew that, even if he pushed his horses only as hard as the Kid pushed his, the advantage was with him. He had three horses, only one of which was bearing any considerable amount of weight. When the horse he was riding became too tired, he could switch to the barebacked one. And when that one became too tired, he could switch the packsaddle to the first one and ride the one that had been carrying it. When the Kid's horses gave out and had to be killed, his should still be very much alive. At least two out of the three should be.

Beyond the crest of the ridge was a gentle slope and after that a wide, flat valley in which a veritable forest of yucca grew. Some of the plants were small, a foot high or less. But some were ancient, taller than a rider's head.

Now, in midday, dust devils danced and whirled across the land. Some towered into the still, dry air as much as a couple of hundred feet. Then, almost as quickly as they had appeared, they would disappear and the dust they left hanging in the air would settle slowly to the ground.

He caught himself thinking about Nora again, and when he closed his eyes he could see her as plainly as if she stood in front of him. Her hair was as black as the wing of a raven and equally shiny when she finished brushing it at night. Her face and neck and arms, while they didn't exactly tan, weren't the bright red associated with sunburn. Rather they were a shade between sunburn and tan and there was a liberal sprinkling of freckles across the bridge of her nose. Her body, where the sun never got to it, was as white as milk and shaped in a way . . . He clenched his shaking hands.

Her eyes were dark and warm, her mouth full. It had a kind of impudent sweetness about it even when it didn't wear a smile. She stood much shorter than he, but could kiss him on the mouth by standing on tiptoe.

There was suddenly an ache in his chest from thinking of her and picturing her in his mind. He thought desperately, 'How can she stand it for as long as she must? She hasn't been on a horse more than three or four hours in the last six months.'

And then he remembered that certain look that sometimes came to Nora's eyes. Determination. Stubbornness. And he knew she'd stand it, until her seat and thighs had hardened to the constant motion of the horse. If the Kid didn't kill her on a reasonless whim, she'd be alive when he caught up.

Or so he stubbornly told himself. But in the back of his mind he kept remembering how long it had taken him and half a dozen Apache scouts to catch up with the Kid before. A month and a half. Of constant riding, of wearing out and killing horses, of going without food, and water, because getting it meant leaving the trail and going a few miles out of the way. He'd lost fifteen pounds himself during that chase, fifteen pounds off a frame that already was about as spare as it could get.

The truth was, and he knew this in some deep recess of his mind, there was little chance he would catch the Kid at all, let alone catch him before he wore Nora out and murdered her. But he shoved these doubts back down into their deep recesses every time they threatened to surface. He couldn't afford to have doubts. If he let himself think of what might happen to Nora, he'd go out of his mind.

Once, he withdrew the Spencer carbine from its saddle boot. He checked its loads, then returned it to the saddle boot. He checked his revolver similarly, replaced it, then checked in his saddlebags to make sure he had enough spare ammunition for both guns. He had a dozen cartridges for the Spencer, maybe twenty for the revolver. Enough. When he came to grips with the Kid he'd be lucky if he got off more than a shot or two.

He had left his ranch at five. Now, at noon, he began to scan the landscape ahead of him with more care than before. The Kid's trail when he left with Nora had been six or seven hours old. He should soon reach the place where the Kid had camped last night, unless, of course, the Kid had continued on.

He held his breath every time he went over the crest of a ridge or knoll, because while he believed the Kid would keep Nora with him, he could never be sure of anything the Kid might do. He knew it was possible he would find Nora staked out naked on an anthill, or bound with a band of rawhide drying around her head, or simply lying in a welter of her own blood with her lovely throat slashed.

Healy realized he was praying softly to himself as he pounded along. Already he was forty-five or fifty miles from home. And then, so suddenly it took him by surprise, he came down into a little draw and was right in the middle of the Apache Kid's last night's camp.

He felt himself go weak with relief because Nora wasn't here. Then his first guess had been right. The Kid didn't intend killing her, at least not right away. As long as she could keep up, please him and do his work, her life was safe.

He left his horses standing and cast about like a hound, bent, stepping carefully, missing nothing on the ground. He found the place where Nora had spent the night, tied hand and foot with leather strips. He found where the Kid had slept, nearly fifty feet away, up on a slight hillside and behind some rocks. The two horses had been tied to a scrub tree as their droppings testified.

He returned to the place where Nora had been and suddenly he saw something on the ground nearly hidden beneath a bush that made tears burn behind his eyes. Nora had drawn a tiny heart in the dirt with an 'N' on one side, an 'F' on the other. It was the only message she could send to him that would mean anything and to Frank Healy, this simple message meant everything. It meant she was all right. It meant she loved him and would remain strong until he could rescue her.

Having scanned the ground and read the tracks, Healy now changed his saddle to the horse that had so far traveled barebacked. He tied his own saddle horse to the tail of the pack animal where the barebacked horse had been tied before. Then he mounted, spurred forcefully and rode away from the site of the Kid's last night's camp at a run.

The terrain was varied now. On most of the north slopes there was grass, while on the south slopes, or those facing south, the ground was all but bare and only cactus grew. The trail led west steadily, with little variation, which led Healy to believe that the Kid had some destination in mind. Perhaps he was headed for a place he knew he could replace his mounts. Healy could think of no other destination that might interest him.

Riding at a run, he let himself think of Nora again, while keeping his eyes on the easily followed tracks of the horses ridden by Nora and the Apache Kid. When he conjured up her face, he saw twinkling eyes and a mocking, impudent smile. When she looked at him like that he always found some excuse to send Francisco and his wife outside and then chased Nora around the house, a chase that always ended upstairs in bed. He felt the urgent need for her suddenly and remembered where she was, and he felt more pure hatred for the Kid than he had ever felt for another human being. He promised himself one thing. If he did not catch up in time, if the Kid killed her, then he'd devote as much of his life afterward as was necessary to catch the Kid. Only this time, the Indian bureau and the Army wouldn't get a chance to send the Kid to prison in Florida. He'd kill the Apache Kid himself and pack the body in, so that never afterward would the Kid be able to kill or terrorize anyone.

The afternoon waned and the sun sank slowly in the western sky. The heat increased. All three of Healy's horses were lathered but he would not rest them because he knew the Apache Kid was not resting his. Only by using his horses ruthlessly as the Kid used his could he ever hope to catch up. Only by killing his horses as the Kid killed his could he hope to save Nora before her strength gave out.

He caught himself remembering her the way she had been when he'd first come to Fort Chiricahua nine years before. He'd come from Fort Apache, where he'd learned the art of trailing, of reading ground on which most men saw nothing, from a white scout named Jake Hanley and from an Apache scout named Nogal. Before he left Fort Apache for Fort Chiricahua, he had been nearly as good as Nogal, and just as good as Hanley was.

Nine years ago. Nora Corcoran had been a leggy girl, a little more than twelve years ago. The first time he'd seen her she was rolling around in the dust of the parade, fighting with a boy about her age and size and beating him to the delighted cheers of half a dozen kids and maybe a dozen troopers who were watching the fight.

The fight had been broken up by the officer

of the day, with a scolding directed mostly at the boy for fighting with a girl. For an instant, as Frank Healy sat his horse looking down, the girl's large, dark eyes had met his squarely and the glance had held for what seemed an eternity. It was Healy who first had looked away and when he glanced back at her he had seen, for the first time, that teasing, impudent smile that he now had grown to know so well.

She told him later, after they were married, that she had picked him out right then. She made up her mind in that instant that she was going to marry him.

When she turned and walked away, it was with her head high and an air of assurance about her that made his glance follow her until she disappeared into her father's house on the far side of the parade.

That was the last fight she had, or at least the last one anybody knew about. She began letting her hair grow long that day. She began pestering Mike Corcoran to let Mrs. Larrabee make her a dress or two. Grown-up dresses. And when Healy saw her in one of them he didn't even recognize the parade ground brawler because Nora was mature for her age and her breasts were already beginning to fill out her dress.

He caught himself grinning as he remembered how often afterward he had seen her, or bumped into her as he went about his business at the fort. Even so, it was a year before he even knew her name, another year before he knew Mike Corcoran was her father and that her mother, who had been Mexican, was dead.

But Nora's determination and stubbornness never wavered. She had made up her mind she was going to marry him. That determination never weakened in the seven years that followed, although it didn't take Healy all those seven years to notice how she had matured. By the time she was eighteen, she was a woman grown, a fact no man could miss. She attended dances at the post. And no matter who her escort was, she always managed, a couple of times during the evening, to be standing in front of Frank Healy as the band began to play.

He knew she was a woman grown the first time he held her in his arms. He remembered grinning as he looked down at her and asked, 'Is this the tomboy I saw fighting on the parade ground the day I first arrived?' And he remembered that now familiar teasing, impudent smile as she replied, 'Oh my, that was just years ago. Do I look like a tomboy now?'

The attraction between them grew slowly because while Nora might have made up her mind, Healy had not. He had no intention of getting married and settling down. He liked his life, liked the association of other men, liked the vastness of the land and the challenge presented by his job. But his mind was finally made up before he went out on the last campaign, which was the pursuit of the Apache Kid.

He asked her when she came to tell him goodbye. The Apache scouts, including Nogal, were ready and waiting. The Kid had left a trail away from Pomeroy's Station where he'd killed two men and stolen a couple of horses and a gun. Healy looked down at her and said, 'I'm damn near old enough to be your pa.'

She smiled sweetly up at him. 'But you're not my pa. Are you?'

'No.' He groped for words, for the first time flustered by those great dark eyes. He finally said, 'A man can't scout forever. Best to quit before somebody tells him he's got to quit. Or before he gets careless and gets himself killed.'

Her great brown eyes didn't waver. She said, 'If you're trying to ask me to marry you, the answer is yes. My goodness, I thought you'd never get around to it.'

That took him by surprise and it was an instant before he recovered his composure. When he did, a wide smile spread across his face. Forgetting the half-dozen Apache scouts waiting for him, he took her in his arms and kissed her hard and long. When he released her, the mockery had gone from her eyes and the smile had gone from her lips. In their place was something else, something he'd never be able to describe but something he would never be able to forget. It was a look in which all the things she felt for him were bared, a look that was naked and vulnerable and loving all at once.

The scouts were snickering so he let her go and climbed on his horse. He called back, 'When I get back from this one I'll resign. I've got a place picked out over in New Mexico. You think you can be ready to go that soon?'

Her smile came back. 'I'll be ready, Mister Frank Healy. Don't you worry about that.'

And ready she was. When he and the Apache scouts came back with the Kid in chains, she was packed and ready to go. She told Mike Corcoran goodbye and Healy assured him there was a place for him on the ranch whenever he got tired of Army life. They drove away in a buckboard Healy had bought, trailing the two saddle horses he owned behind.

The two years of their marriage had seemed more like two weeks. And now she was gone, in the hands of an Apache killing machine, no more than a quick breath away from death at any time, night or day.

CHAPTER THREE

Nora Healy was upstairs making the bed she shared with her husband when she heard the dog barking furiously in the yard. She reached the window in time to see the dog standing stiff-legged, every hair on his neck and back erect. Her eyes followed the direction of the dog's glance and she saw an Apache approaching the house at a trot. He was on foot, and carried a short, trapdoor, single-shot rifle in his left hand. When he was within a dozen yards of the dog, the animal rushed, snarling and snapping. Like light the Apache's hand snatched a knife from its sheath at his side. The dog leaped, the knife sank into his side and the dog fell back to the ground. Calmly, the Apache stooped, withdrew the knife and wiped its blade on the dog's side. He did not replace it in its sheath, but came on toward the house.

There was no gun in the upstairs bedroom, nothing with which Nora could successfully defend herself. But Francisco and María were down in the kitchen. Nora hurried to the head of the stairs and screamed, 'Francisco! María! There's an Indian coming! He just killed the dog!'

Even as the last of her warning scream rang out, she knew it had come too late. She heard a violent commotion in the kitchen, chairs overturning, dishes breaking, grunts of exertion from Francisco and the cries of terror from María. Then only silence.

Nora had grown up at Fort Chiricahua and was used to seeing Apaches, both the scouts employed by the Army and the renegades that were sometimes brought to the fort after capture. They did not all look alike to her as they did to many whites.

She had recognized the Indian crossing the yard. He was supposed to be imprisoned in Florida but he was here, downstairs in the kitchen. And he had just killed both Francisco and María. She couldn't hear him now but she knew that he had probably already begun searching the house for her.

It crossed her mind that she should hide, but she knew it would do no good. The Apache Kid would find her no matter where she hid. Nor would it help her to put up a fight. That might anger him and if she angered him she also would most certainly be killed.

She was probably going to be murdered anyway. Her husband Frank had been in charge of the Apache scouts who caught the Apache Kid two years ago. He must have escaped from the Florida prison, she thought. He had to have escaped. He would certainly not have been released. Not with *his* record of cold-blooded mass murder.

She stood in the bedroom doorway, facing the stairs. If he meant to kill her he would kill her. But he might have something else in mind. He might intend to kidnap her, take her along with him to do his cooking and firewood gathering as he had, in the past, taken Apache women from their villages. If that was his intention then her life would be spared for now. But when her strength failed and she could no longer do his work, when she could no longer keep up the murderous grueling pace, *then* he would kill her just as he had killed at least half a dozen women before.

She saw his face at the foot of the stairs. It was a youngish face, smooth and unlined and very dark. His shoulder-length hair was black and straight, bound at his forehead with a faded red piece of cloth. He wore a faded blue Army shirt, breechclout and typical Apache high-topped moccasins. He still held the short rifle in his left hand, the bloodstained knife in his right. The front of his legs and his breechclout were spattered with blood. Francisco's blood, she thought.

She wanted to launch herself at him the way she'd often launched herself at a boy who had been tormenting her. She wanted to scream 'murderer!' at him, but she made no sound. For nearly a minute they stared at each other silently. Finally he said, in Spanish, which she understood, 'You come. You my woman now.'

Going obediently down the stairs was the hardest thing she had ever done. He turned his back on her, seeming to know she would not dare to do him harm. Or maybe his sense of hearing was so keen he knew he would hear her long before she could get to him.

She stared with horror at the scene in the kitchen. María must have died quietly. She lay sprawled out flat on the floor, a large pool of blood beneath the deep slash in her throat. Francisco had fought. Even after the fatal wound had been administered he had fought, in much the same way a chicken flops aimlessly after its head has been severed by an ax. Blood was spattered everywhere, on furniture, walls and floor. And, Nora recalled, on the Apache Kid's breechclout and legs.

She was weeping when she stepped through the kitchen door and into the yard. Weeping for María and Francisco. Weeping for the horror and senselessness of what the Apache Kid had done. He gave her a cold, expressionless stare. In Spanish he said, 'I get horses. You get food.'

She wasn't sure she could face going back into the kitchen but she knew better than to refuse. The Kid crossed the yard toward the corral. Nora went into the house.

Her eyes went instantly to the corner of the kitchen where Francisco's shotgun always leaned. It wasn't there. Its smashed pieces lay near Francisco's body.

And there weren't any other guns. Frank had a revolver and a Spencer repeating rifle, but he always carried them with him when he was away from the house.

The trouble was, she thought as she began absently gathering a flour sack full of food, they'd felt safe here in western New Mexico. It had been years since Apaches had raided this far east.

They simply hadn't counted on the Apache Kid. They hadn't counted on his terrible, unquenched thirst for vengeance. The Apache Kid killed, for the most part, without feeling of any kind. But he *hated* Frank Healy. And he hated all the Apache scouts who, with Frank Healy, had pursued him deep into Mexico and brought him back to be imprisoned for his crimes.

She couldn't remember the names of all the scouts. Only one, who had been Frank's friend. His name was Nogal. She wondered if the Kid had killed Nogal before coming here. Faintly she shook her head. Frank would have been first on the Kid's death list. Only after Frank was dead would the Kid go after the Apache scouts.

It seemed sacrilegious to leave the bodies of María and Francisco lying there. Then she realized that Frank would be coming home tonight. He wouldn't be able to trail in darkness so he'd use the time to bury Francisco and his wife. And the dog, of whom they both had been genuinely fond.

She left the kitchen carrying a partially filled flour sack as the Apache Kid came from the corral leading two horses, one saddled. He gestured with his head for her to follow and she did. Her Irish temper was at a fever pitch and it was nearly impossible for her to meekly obey this killer's contemptuous commands. But she was thinking of Frank. And she was very much aware that the first time she failed to do the Apache Kid's bidding, or failed to please him in any way, or slowed him down, or showed anger or weariness, he'd kill her as quickly, unfeelingly and efficiently as he had killed Francisco and María Martínez.

For Frank, then, she must stay alive. For Frank, who could trail and catch the Apache Kid if anyone could in the whole Southwest. He had done it once and he could do it again.

About a quarter mile from the house they came to the body of a horse. The animal's hair was lathered and his throat was cut.

The Kid took his Apache saddle off the horse and put it on the barebacked one he had brought from the corral. In Spanish, Nora asked, 'How did you get out of the prison in Florida?'

He did not reply. He just looked at her, with a mixture of dislike and contempt. With his head, he gestured for her to mount. She did.

In Spanish he said, as he led out, 'You keep up or I kill you.'

It was a simple statement whose tone of voice was in no way threatening. Nora knew it was a strict statement of fact.

The Kid let out a wild yell that scared the horse he was riding into a lope. He let out another, similar yell, at the same time belaboring the horse's rump with the short barrel of his trapdoor 45–70. The horse, fresh anyway and eager, immediately began to run.

Nora's horse fell behind for the first three or four hundred feet. She had nothing with which to hit him on the rump, but she drummed her heels against his sides, raking his flanks with her heels. Flanking him might make him buck but she didn't think so. Not with the other horse at a dead run ahead of him.

The Kid's horse started up a rocky incline, lunging. He necessarily slowed because of the terrain, and Nora's horse caught up. The Kid did not look around at her. She thought, 'Oh God, if I only had a gun.' Yet somehow she knew that even if she did, even if she got it out and pointed it at the back of the Apache Kid, he'd somehow know and would turn and kill her before she had a chance to fire.

Nora's stirrups were too long. They were Francisco's length and she couldn't reach them with her feet.

Long stirrups that she couldn't reach didn't mean she couldn't ride or stay on the horse. They only meant less comfort and more rubbing of her thighs against the saddle skirt. Nora was an expert horsewoman, having begun riding at age four when Mike Corcoran put her up on one of the great, tall cavalry remounts from whose back the distance to the ground looked like a hundred feet. But she hadn't ridden a horse in months. And she knew that both her seat and the insides of her thighs would rub, turn red, blister and eventually become unendurable. Unless she did something.

She hauled her horse to a halt. She knew full

well that the Kid might come back and kill her. But she also knew that if she did not now protect her thighs, she would eventually be unable to continue and he would kill her anyway.

She dismounted from her horse instantly she had brought him to a stop. She sat down on the ground, without even looking at the Apache Kid, and began tearing wide strips from her petticoat. She tried not to expose any more leg than she had to because she knew a display of white thighs might well inflame the Kid and bring on the thing that, next to death, she dreaded most.

The Kid seemed to have known the instant that she stopped. He turned his horse and came back, a murderous scowl on his face, his eyes like black bits of stone. In English this time he said, 'Goddamn you woman! I gonna kill you now.'

Nora did not look up. The strips were torn from her petticoat and she was busily rolling them. When she had finished, she pulled up her dress and petticoat and began winding them around her thighs.

She knew that at any instant a bullet might tear into her breast. Or a thrown knife might bury itself in her.

Desperately she wanted to look up but she stubbornly resisted the impulse. Finally she finished, split the bandages and tied them on the outside of her thighs so that they wouldn't rub against the saddle skirt.

She got up, and now she looked at the Apache Kid. 'I'm ready now.' If he understood English she was damned if she was going to speak to him in any other language. She began to readjust the stirrups' length.

His eyes had a strange glow to them, the most expression she had ever seen them show. She recognized that glow, having seen it in the eyes of other men. She got on her horse and waited while he stared at her. She did not meet his glance.

She half expected him to yank her off her horse and rape her right here and now but he did not. He slammed the rifle barrel down on his horse's rump and forced the animal to go lunging up the rocky slope.

Nora lashed her own horse's rump with the ends of the reins and drummed her heels against the horse's sides. It probably wasn't necessary now because the two horses seemed to be working together, wanting to stay together. Later, of course, when both were near exhaustion, her horse would have to be belabored constantly, as would that of the Apache Kid, to keep them moving along as fast as the Kid wanted them to.

The bandages that Nora had wound around her thighs spared them any further chafing. She clung to the saddle horn when necessary going up a hill and braced herself both against the stirrups and against the pommel going down.

The miles fell behind.

In midafternoon, it was very hot. The horses were both heavily lathered but the Kid did not slow them down. Nor did he give them any opportunity to rest. Nora's horse gradually fell behind despite her efforts to force him to keep up.

Finally, the Kid reined in his horse momentarily and waved Nora past. After that, whenever Nora's horse slowed, the Kid whacked him on the rump with a long branch of mesquite he had broken off.

Once they stopped at a trickle of water in the bottom of a ravine. The Kid dismounted and motioned for Nora to follow suit. The horses sucked noisily at the trickle of water. The Kid stared coldly at Nora and finally said, in Spanish, 'Your man come after you.'

She nodded and said in English, 'Yes.'

The Kid said, in English this time. 'He big damn fool. No sense risk life for woman.'

'Just the same, he'll risk it for me. Even if I was dead, he would still hunt you down. Like he did the last time. Only this time you won't go to prison in Florida. You will hang like any white criminal.'

He was on her before the last of the words were out of her mouth. He struck her savagely with the flat of his hand squarely in the mouth. She felt her lips crush and tasted blood.

She stared at him, her Irish temper flaring and showing plainly in her eyes. She didn't flinch and she didn't cringe away.

He met her glance squarely for a long time. She had no idea what he was going to do next. Perhaps he'd kill her outright and have it over with. Perhaps he'd beat her. Perhaps . . .

But he did none of these things. With a curt gesture of his head he directed her to mount. He slashed her horse savagely across the rump with the branch of mesquite. The two horses lunged up out of the ravine, still heading west and now at least twenty-five miles from Frank Healy's ranch.

Nora Healy began to feel a little hope. The Apache Kid knew Frank. He knew Frank could cover just as many miles in a day as he could. He knew Frank could be as ruthless with his horses as any Apache ever born if the stakes were high enough.

And Nora Healy knew the stakes *were* high enough. Even if she hadn't yet told Frank she was almost sure that she was carrying his child.

CHAPTER FOUR

The afternoon hours waned. The sun sank toward the ragged line of rocky ridges to the west. The horses were stumbling now, and once Nora's fell, throwing her forward over his head.

She scratched her arm and banged her head against a rock, painfully but not hard enough to stun her. She got up immediately. The horse was already up, shaking himself. Dust had turned the lather on the horse's side to mud.

She guessed they must have covered nearly sixty miles when the Kid finally halted in the shade of a shallow ravine.

Heat had built in the ravine throughout the day and no breeze stirred. Nora knew nothing of this country, of course, but she felt sure the Kid considered himself to be far enough from the Healy ranch to be safe for the night. Even if Frank had returned home early, left the Martínezes unburied and started immediately, he could not possibly have covered even half the distance she and the Kid had traveled.

There was a trickle of water in the ravine and he motioned her to drink. She did so obediently, drinking as much as she could hold, knowing it might be a long time before she got another drink. Then the Kid motioned her to lie down on the ground.

For a moment, pure terror ran through her. He knelt over her. Every instinct told her to fight. Good sense told her not to show this brutal Indian any resistance at all.

Relief ran through her like a flood when she saw the two short leather thongs he had in his hands. First he tied her feet, then her hands behind her back. He drew up the end of the thong securing her feet and tied it to the thongs that held her hands.

Both horses stood about fifty feet away,

heads hanging, their legs trembling. Nora had expected the Kid to kill them both but he did not.

He unsaddled them and led them to the trickle of water in the ravine. He let them drink, then led them up the ravine a ways and tied them to a scrubby tree. He went up on the hillside, knelt and hollowed out a depression in the ground for his hip. He laid down and promptly went to sleep.

Dusk came rapidly and darkness soon afterward. Nora was exhausted but at first she couldn't sleep. The thongs with which she was tied cut off her circulation. Besides, she could not forget Frank.

Overcome with emotion and with tears filling her eyes, she suddenly and impulsively drew a small heart in the sand beneath the nearest bush, putting an 'N' on one side, an 'F' on the other. Then, smiling faintly because she knew he would find it when he found this place where she had slept, she went to sleep.

It was not a deep or an easy sleep. Her arms and hands pained her and so did her legs and feet. What worried her most was that, when morning came, she wouldn't be able to get up and walk. She wouldn't be able to mount her horse and if she could not do that she would be killed right here.

But there wasn't anything she could do but wait, and hope, and pray.

She was awake when dawn first streaked the

sky. The Kid awoke quickly, simply sitting up and then getting silently to his feet. She had thought he would check the horses first but he did not. He came to her and untied her, then looping the two thongs in another that secured his breechclout around his waist. He left her immediately and went after the horses.

He hadn't seen the heart she'd drawn and the fact that he hadn't gave her hope. It proved he was not infallible. He could make mistakes. And if he could make one he could make more.

She crawled to the stream and got a drink. Then she pushed herself into a sitting position and began to rub her arms and wrists, her ankles and legs. It didn't seem as if she'd ever be able to get up and walk again but when the Kid came back, leading the horses, she made it to her feet. Hurriedly while the Kid was busy with the horses she relieved herself.

Again, she doubted if she'd be able to mount, but mount she did and when the Kid rode out at a merciless, lunging gait up the side of the ravine, she clung to her saddle and stayed immediately behind.

When he reached level ground, coming down out of the rocky, cactus-covered hills and the land stretched away for what seemed like sixty miles, he slowed both horses to a trot, at which gait they faltered less than they had previously.

Wistfully, she looked behind them once, as if hoping that by some miracle she would see

Frank coming, a speck in the distance, but coming all the same. All she saw were the dust devils, whirling, climbing with the rising morning heat from the desert floor into the flawless sky.

She kept rubbing her arms and, when she had restored circulation to them, raised one leg after another and massaged the ankles where the cruel leather thongs had been. She wondered if it would do any good to promise the Kid that she wouldn't try to run away and so avoid being tied every night. She doubted it, but she determined to try it next time they stopped. She didn't know how many nights she could endure being tied the way she had been last night.

They traveled at an alternate trot and walk for about ten miles across the flat. Then, in the distance, Nora saw the outline of some scattered buildings, and she knew this was the Kid's destination, the next place he would get horses, the next place his killing tools would strike.

He found a dry wash that led in the general direction of the buildings and rode his horse down into it. Nora followed. They rode along the wash in almost unendurable heat for about five miles. Then the Kid stopped his horse. He motioned for Nora to dismount. She opened her mouth to protest being tied and he grabbed one of her ankles and yanked her roughly out of her saddle. The fall knocked the wind out of her and for several moments she couldn't speak. By the time she could, she was trussed and the Kid was approaching the two horses, who stood with their heads hanging, their legs trembling.

The Kid drew his knife. When he reached the nearest horse, he plunged the knife into his neck and with a swift downward motion, severed both the horse's windpipe and his jugular. The horse didn't even have the strength to run. He just folded and fell where he had stood.

The Kid killed the second horse the same way, afterward casually wiping the knifeblade on the horse's side the way he had on the Healy's pet dog yesterday.

Nora knew both horses, liked them both, and had ridden both hundreds of times. To see them so casually used up and then slaughtered made a wave of pure hatred like nothing she had ever experienced before wash over her.

Sheathing his knife, the Kid set off at a steady trot and, in seconds, had disappeared.

She wondered how far away the ranch was now. She wondered how long he would be gone. She tried for about five minutes to take off the leather strips with which he'd tied her. At the end of that time she hadn't even loosened them so she gave up.

She knew that the Kid hadn't tied her to prevent her escape. Escape from the Kid was an impossibility. He had tied her only to save himself loss of time pursuing and recapturing her.

Maybe, she thought, those at the ranch would be on guard. Maybe they'd kill the Kid. She'd know that soon, probably within half an hour. He'd either return with fresh horses or he would not return at all.

And if he did not return at all? She'd lie here until those at the ranch backtracked him tomorrow or until Frank came.

Her arms and legs were beginning to hurt again because the circulation in them had been cut off again so soon. She was tired, and hot, and she ached all over. Her seat was sore from the saddle but she *had* managed to spare her thighs by putting bandages on them.

When the Kid came back with fresh mounts, he'd transfer the saddles and they'd be off again. By dark, they might be another fifty miles away.

How in the world had Frank caught the Apache Kid before? And how was he going to catch him now? The Indian could cover a hundred miles in a twenty-four-hour period. He was tough and wiry and seemingly tireless.

But so was Frank. So was Frank, but how about her? She wasn't tough enough, no matter how determined she might be, to last out too many days of this kind of traveling.

Softly she began to pray. That Frank would catch up before her strength gave out. And that the hardship and hard riding would not cause her to abort the child she was now sure had begun to form inside of her.

She heard the horses first. She turned her head and looked in the direction from which the sound came and saw the Kid coming along the wash, riding one horse, leading another. He didn't speak and neither did she. She didn't want to know how many people he had killed to get the two horses but she knew that he had killed. There was fresh blood on his legs and breechclout.

She lay still, feeling again the pure, white-hot hatred flowing through her. He could have gotten the horses without any killing. But he hadn't wanted to.

His hatred must be even stronger than hers, she thought. And then unwillingly she began to understand. Imprisonment, for an Apache, was like caging an eagle. And to be imprisoned in a fetid, humid, tropical place like Florida. She began to wonder how many he had killed for pure revenge effecting his escape and how many on the long journey west.

Whatever his reasons, whatever he thought was his justification, it had nothing to do with the innocent people he was killing now. They didn't even know who he was. They probably had never even heard of him.

He came to her, rolled her over ungently, and began working on the knots that tied her hands and feet. There was plenty of opportunity, but his hands did not touch her except as necessary to untie the thongs. She caught a glimpse of his face, once, and it was expressionless except for its intent look.

Only once had she seen a look of lust in his eyes and that had been while her thighs were necessarily exposed for bandaging. If she was careful and provided no further provocation, perhaps he would not molest her at all. He must be tired despite the fact that he showed no sign of weariness. And she knew he was intent on leading her husband back and forth across Arizona until he had worn Frank down enough to cause Frank to make one, small, fatal mistake.

The last of the thongs, those around her ankles, dropped away. He looped them around the one that supported his breechclout and knotted them once. He grabbed her arm and yanked her to her feet.

She could hardly stand, so badly had the circulation been cut off from her legs. She rubbed her arms and hobbled toward the horse the Kid had indicated would be hers. She mounted. Once mounted and feeling the sense of safety that went with being on horseback she asked, bitterness plain in her voice, 'How many did you kill back there? How many for these two horses?'

She spoke in English, knowing he understood, but he neither answered her nor turned his head. She was wasting both her breath and her anger, she realized. As useful to be angry at the coyote who ravages through a flock of sheep, slashing throats and killing thirty or forty for the pure pleasure of it when all he could possibly eat would be one.

The Kid rode off at a reckless gallop. Nora raked her own horse's sides with her heels and belabored him with the ends of the reins. She finally managed to reach and maintain a position fifty feet behind the Kid.

Apparently he could hear her horse because he didn't look around.

Nora had learned a lot of profane words from the boys at Fort Chiricahua while she was growing up. Now she found some small satisfaction in cursing the Apache Kid under her breath. And in promising him a slow death, Apache style, when Frank caught up.

But all the time she knew that Frank was probably not going to catch up, at least not while she was alive. The Apache Kid would wait until she gave out. Then he'd kill her in such a way that the sight of her body would drive Frank literally out of his mind when he came upon what was left of her. The Kid would be waiting there, knowing all Frank's cunning, learned from the Apaches themselves, all his common sense and skill would go flying when he saw the body of his wife.

The situation seemed hopeless, as nothing had ever seemed hopeless to Nora Healy before. But she told herself determinedly it was only hopeless if she let it be. If she remained strong, she could count on Frank to pursue either until he was dead or until he had killed the Kid.

But, oh Lord, what if it rained? What if high winds wiped out the trail? What if the Kid put 'Apache horseshoes' made of rawhide from either cow or horsehide on the feet of the mounts they rode?

She firmed her mouth and clenched her teeth. She wasn't going to think of the things that might happen to make Frank fail. Frank wasn't going to fail. Without that belief, her own strength could not possibly last.

The horses the Kid had stolen this time were not the tough, short-legged ponies so common on the western plains. They were light work horses, used for pulling a buckboard or spring wagon, or for light garden plowing around the house. They had neither the speed nor the stamina of the two horses the Kid had stolen out of Frank Healy's corral. Maybe, please God, they'd travel slower than the horses her husband had.

Nora's mother had been a good Catholic. Her father had told her that often enough. Himself, being Irish, had been Catholic but because of the kind of man he was, an indifferent one. Between them, though, they had taught her to believe in God.

Now in spite of herself, her faith wavered. What kind of God would let a killing machine like the Apache Kid rampage back and forth over Arizona Territory murdering innocent people like the Martínezes and the ranchers from whom he had stolen these light work horses they were riding now? If there was a God why didn't he strike this monster down?

Her teachings gave her no answer for these questions, of course. But she knew one thing above all else. In her situation, she could not rely on God. She must rely on herself, trusting in God only to make her strength hold out. And she must rely on Frank, trusting God only to give him the stamina and the skill to run the Apache Kid to earth again before it was too late.

CHAPTER FIVE

Frank Healy reached the wide flat that Nora had thought to be sixty miles across in midafternoon. It was not that broad but it *was* half that distance across and once, in prehistoric times, had been the bed of a lake. Fossils of marine organisms could still be found imbedded in layers of sandstone, including skeletal fish as much as three inches long.

He took to the arroyo when the trail of the Kid did, and followed it galloping recklessly. According to his calculations, he was now no more than four hours behind.

He had not missed the buildings in the

distance, and he understood what had been in the mind of the Apache Kid when he left the level plain for the concealment of the dry arroyo. He meant to get horses at the ranch. Healy would find the two horses the Kid had stolen from his own corral lying in the arroyo with their throats cut, used up and nearly dead before the Kid ever touched a knife to them.

And he had recognized the collection of buildings. Known as Slattery's, it was a working ranch upon which Slattery ran about two hundred head of long-horned Mexican cattle. It was also a store, a road-house, where liquor and food were served, and an overnight stop for casual travelers.

The horse Healy was riding was heavily lathered and beginning to stumble every few hundred yards. Reluctantly he halted, dismounted and changed his saddle to the bare-backed horse tied to the packhorse's tail. He then replaced the worn-out horse at the rear of the line, cinched the saddle down, mounted and spurred out again at a lope.

He saw the bodies of the horses first. He halted when he was still a couple of hundred yards away and approached on foot, studying the ground carefully as he walked.

He saw where the Kid had stopped. He saw where he had pushed Nora to the ground, where he had knelt and tied her hands and feet. He went on, following the Kid's moccasin tracks to where he had stopped long enough to slit both horses' throats. Then, seeing that the tracks now headed for Slattery's, he went back and got his horses, mounted and followed the Kid's moccasin tracks up out of the arroyo.

The Kid now had done what any Apache does best. It was doubtful if anyone at Slattery's had even seen him until he burst in through the door. He had run, crept or crawled from brush clump to brush clump until he was within fifty yards of Slattery's on the blind side where the hay barn sheltered him from view of the house. Then he had run in openly, pausing at the corner of the barn, then rushing for the door of the house, at top speed.

Frank called, 'Hey! Anybody here? I'm Frank Healy and I'm trailing the Apache Kid!'

There was no reply from Slattery's. He rode toward the house, noting that the corral gate stood open wide and that half a dozen horses were grouped uncertainly near the base of the windmill where there was water in an algae-filled, galvanized tank.

Long before he reached the door, he knew what he was going to find. The question was, how many? That depended on how many people had been present at Slattery's. Ordinarily, there was only Slattery himself, a man of sixty, with a nearly white beard and a thick mane of hair. Slattery was built like a Sonora bull, with slim hips and powerful shoulders. His neck was short and thick. Given fair warning, and a knife himself, he might have been a match for the Apache Kid. But he'd had no warning and no knife. He had been stabbed in the back by a swiftly rushing Apache Kid and had probably felt only a brief burning sensation before death came to him.

A second occupant was Slattery's Mexican woman. She had been plump and agreeable and thirty years younger then Slattery. She'd taken good care of him and had done the woman's work that needed to be done around the place. Her eyes were wide with terror and there was a bloodstain as big as Healy's hand between her ample breasts. Gently he closed her eyes and folded her hands across her breast.

Healy knew he ought to stay and bury them. He also knew that he would not. Nor would either of them want him to. Their wanton murders cried out to be avenged.

Healy had always hated the Kid but his hatred, bitter and savage as it already was, still could keep growing with every atrocity he had to see.

He went out, not bothering to close the door. He mounted, drove the loose horses into the corral and closed the gate. There were two he thought had stamina and sufficient speed. He caught them, transferred his saddle to one, the packsaddle to the second one. The horse he was riding he returned to the end of the string, tying his halter rope to the tail of the horse now bearing the pack. He left the corral gate ajar.

These were not fast riding horses, but were light work horses, used for pulling buckboards, spring wagons and the mud wagons that occasionally passed through here. But they were the same kind of horses the Kid now had. Healy had vertified that by studying the tracks.

Leaving two of his own worn-out horses behind, he took the Apache Kid's trail back to the arroyo. He picked it up again, spurring and belaboring the horse he was riding across the rump with his Spencer to make the animal move faster.

The trail turned north toward the nearest of the purple hills. By now it was getting along toward late afternoon and the hills had assumed a shade that was a combination of lavender and pink.

Frank Healy tried to calculate the hours of daylight left to him. He dragged out his old silver watch. He had forgotten to wind it the night before and silently cursed his own stupidity. But he was almost as used to telling time without a watch as he was *with* one and he guessed it was a little after four o'clock.

At this time of year, the sun set between seven and seven-thirty, and for fifteen minutes after sundown it remained light enough to trail. That gave him nearly three and a half hours.

He spurred and slashed his horse's rump with the reins until he got him to maintain a steady lope. He could tell from the tracks that the Kid was maintaining a similar gait. Nora was probably fifty or a hundred feet behind and he was sure she knew better than to fall any farther behind than that.

Frank's own saddle horse was now running bare-backed behind the packhorse, wearing a halter the rope of which was tied to the packhorse's tail. Frank turned his head and studied the way the horse moved.

Even without a load, the horse was weakening. He had traveled too long, too far, and he'd had neither enough to eat nor enough water to replace that sweated out by the murderous heat and pace.

The horse might make it, Frank thought, if he turned him loose now. He might make his way back home but the chances were pretty good that Frank would never see him again.

He liked the horse, but he knew he wasn't going to turn him loose. The horse might make ten minutes' difference in the distance between him and the Apache Kid. Or half an hour or two minutes. Any amount would be worthwhile but when Frank finally caught up with the Kid, this horse was one more thing for which he was going to have to pay.

Travel here, on this wide flat, was easier than in the hills. The trail was plain, and Frank didn't even have to concentrate. It was almost as though the Kid was deliberately leaving a plain and easily followed trail so that Frank Healy would have more time to think.

And think he did. His mind remembered

Nora the way he had left her that last morning, fresh in a gingham gown, her hair drawn up and formed into a knot high on her head so that it would be out of her way while she worked. When it was up like that, her white throat and neck were visible and he liked to run his fingers around beneath her ears just to hear her squeals of protest because he tickled her.

What must she look like now? No longer would her hair be up in a bun because she would need its protection from the sun. It would be down around her shoulders, and tangled because she had no comb and perhaps would even contain small twigs and burrs.

Her lovely face would be scratched by unavoidable contact with the long branches of ocotillo or mesquite. It would be sunburned now, bright red, and her nose would be peeling and perhaps blistering. And because the Kid kept her riding steadily all day and tied all night, she'd have little or no opportunity to try and make herself some kind of hat out of a slender branch formed into a circle and covered with part of her dress or petticoat.

And what about the rest of her? She wasn't used to riding. Her seat and thighs must be raw by now. Every joint and muscle in her body must ache ferociously with every movement of the horse.

Oh God, how tough was she? How *really* tough was she? Tough enough never to give up no matter what punishment her body had to endure? Or would she reach a point where she would simply prefer death to continuing?

Frank had never felt so defeated and frustrated in his life before. The one dearest to him in all the world was a scant thirty or forty miles ahead and there was nothing he could do that he wasn't already doing to close the gap.

He felt like shouting, like raving, and then he thought of Nora, who must endure silently or risk being killed. He drew the carbine from its saddle boot and began to belabor the hard-galloping horse on the rump.

At about five, he reached the far edge of the flat, and once more the trail climbed into the hills. Now Frank considered a new hazard, which was that the Kid had found himself a hiding place, had watched Frank ride toward him across the plain, intent on the trail and little else. Nothing would be simpler for him than to ambush Frank, shoot only to wound and then force him to watch while he tortured and killed Nora.

After that, he could satisfy his lust for vengeance by making Frank's own death as slow and as painful as possible.

He shook his head. He didn't think the Kid was ready yet for that. The Kid wanted Frank to suffer more and he wanted Nora to suffer more. He wanted them both at the edge of exhaustion when the final showdown came.

No. He figured if the Kid did ambush him he'd shoot the horse he was riding and both of the others if he could. He would try leaving Frank afoot, knowing that while he plodded along the Kid and Nora were drawing even farther and farther away, hopelessly out of reach.

Having decided what the Kid's next move would likely be, Frank immediately dismounted and once more changed the worn-out saddle horse at the end of the string. He saddled him, mounted, and went on up the slope, still following the trail, but now more alert than he had ever been in his life before.

He was prepared to sacrifice the horse he was riding. He had already given up on that one's life. He was gambling that, expecting this action from the Kid, his reflexes might be fast enough to prevent the Kid from killing the other two.

The shot, even though expected, still startled and made him jerk. But he was off the horse's back before the echo died away. The horse he had been riding was folding already, but Healy paid no attention to him. He was facing toward the other two horses, waving his arms and screeching like a Comanche. He scooped up a handful of gravel and threw it into the lead horse's face, partially blinding him. The horse turned, slammed into the one behind, then ran parallel to the hillside. The Kid fired again, but Healy was ready this time and fired his own Spencer at the powder burst. Then he dived for cover, knowing the Kid's third shot would take him in the chest if he did not.

He hit the rocky ground behind a good-sized clump of prickly pear and waited, hoping the Kid would buy the ruse that he had been hit. He glanced in the direction his two horses had gone, relieved to see that they had disappeared into a deep washout fifty feet away.

Now, with the Kid less than a dozen yards from him, he had the first decent chance he'd had to come to grips with him and get Nora back. Recklessly, without a second thought, he leaped to his feet and charged up the hillside. In all no more than a minute had elapsed since the Kid's first bullet went through his horse's neck.

But all he saw was the rump of the Kid's horse disappearing over the crest of the ridge, now some fifty or sixty feet away. He knew it was no use, but he ran with all the speed of which he was capable to the top, readying himself to shoot.

Long before he reached the crest, he suspected the Kid had outsmarted him. He was not mistaken. Nora sat on her horse more than half a mile away. Her horse was apparently tied to a clump of mesquite. She was looking toward him but the distance was too great to see what her expression was. The Kid was about halfway between by now, his horse at a dead run.

The distance was too great but Healy's frustration was unbearable. He knelt, got the best bead he could on the Kid and his horse, and fired.

He missed, and saw dust kick up behind the Kid where the bullet struck. Knowing a second shot was useless, he turned and ran back down to where his horses stood. He had frightened them, and they were hard to catch. Furthermore, he had to transfer his saddle from the dead horse to the barebacked one. By the time he reached the crest of the ridge a second time, both the Kid and Nora had disappeared.

Healy had never cursed so long or bitterly in his life before. The Kid and Nora had been so close. And he'd let them get away!

CHAPTER SIX

Healy was fuming as he rode past the body of his dead horse. But his mind was beginning to work again. The Kid had planned this in exactly the way it had happened. Nora, bound hand and foot, and mounted, had been helpless half a mile away, her horse securely tied. He'd never had a chance to rescue her.

Nor had his chance of killing the Kid been much better. The Kid had been after his horses and Healy had known he had to protect them from the Kid's bullets or be left out here afoot, something that would have been intolerable.

But hardly more intolerable, he told himself,

than to actually be within a dozen yards of the Kid and be too busy to kill him. Damn!

Yet deep within himself he knew he'd moved just as fast as a man can move. He had done his best. No one could have done more. Time after time in the past the Apache Kid had laid similar ambushes, but this time he'd succeeded in killing but one of Healy's mounts—a worn-out one at that. And he'd gained no ground. He'd lost ground in fact, a lot of it, while he waited at the crest of the ridge for Healy to come in range.

Healy had hoped he might get another glimpse of Nora and the Kid before darkness fell, but he did not. At last he was forced to stop.

Tonight he knew that, unless the Kid kept moving through a good part of the night, they'd spend it within two or three miles of each other. And he knew the Kid well enough to be sure that he would not let the opportunity such closeness presented to be ignored.

He made camp in a deep ravine. He tied his two horses in a clump of paloverde, using his lariat to form a kind of fence around three sides of it. He himself found a place to wait fifty feet from the open end of the corral thus formed. He checked his Spencer's loads and those of his revolver and sat down.

The Kid wasn't likely to leave this place without trying to kill his horses, of that Healy felt sure. And when the Kid came to kill his horses then he would have a chance to kill the Kid himself.

But as he sat and waited, another possibility occurred to him. Maybe the Kid didn't intend trying to kill his horses a second time. Maybe, knowing Healy would stay awake all night because he expected it, he'd travel on, and by morning be fifty miles away. He wouldn't have had any sleep, but then Healy would have spent the night sleeplessly too.

Damn a sly Apache anyway! You had to out think them all the time, and most times you failed. Fighting them was never simple. Fighting an Apache was always more slyness than it was hand-to-hand combat.

You could never choose the conditions under which you fought. The Apache did that. You played by the Apache's rules and you had to be smarter and tougher and a better fighter all around. That was why so many white people's bones lay moldering beneath the Arizona desert soil.

Healy had found a place to sit from which he could clearly see the clump of paloverde trees. There still remained enough light in the sky to see the darker shapes of the horses, and he could hear them moving around.

He laid the Spencer across his lap, and now tried to remember enough about that hasty glimpse he'd had of Nora to tell whether she had still seemed strong or not.

The distance had been great, more than half

a mile. He'd had no time to study her because he'd been looking for the Kid, hoping for a killing shot. Damn it, he thought, he couldn't even remember whether she'd seemed strong or not. He just hadn't gotten that close a look at her. And besides, distance had defeated him. She'd been too far away even to recognize her unless he'd already known who she was.

He heard a distant rumble, so faint he could almost convince himself he had imagined it. But he knew he had not because, when his glance turned east, he saw a faint, orange-colored flare just above the horizon. Nearly two minutes later, he heard a second rumble of thunder.

Fate seemed to be favoring the Apache Kid, he thought bitterly. This part of Arizona usually went for months without a thunderstorm. But it was going to get one now. And the rain would wipe out the trail Nora and the Kid had made.

He waited until the rain began and long after before he dared let himself relax. As tired as he was, it was only a matter of minutes before he was sound asleep.

He had no idea how long he slept. It must have been for several hours because when he awoke thunder was rumbling directly overhead, and lightning was flashing every half minute or so.

He had seldom experienced such discouragement. In the dry desert soil, the trail would be wiped completely out. He had nothing with which to start in the morning. Nothing but a mud-washed landscape as barren of tracks as would have been the moon.

The sky was still as black as pitch. Healy's blanket was soaked. He lay there in uncomfortable wetness for several minutes before he finally got up in disgust. He shook his blanket out and rolled it up into a tight roll. He wrung it, even though doing so brought out only a limited amount of water. Draping it over a clump of brush, he made his way to where the horses were.

He'd made no mistake in sleeping, because the two horses still were there, soaked and uncomfortable. He selected the one he intended to ride and put a bridle on him. He led him out, put on the soggy saddle blanket and followed that with the saddle. He cinched it down.

Having saddled the horse he would ride, he put the soggy pad on the packhorse and followed it with the packsaddle, upon which he hung the loaded panniers. The saddles on their backs warmed both horses and before long they stopped shivering. Healy waited, keeping an eye on the eastern horizon, looking for the gray of dawn.

The rain turned to hail, which ripped the leaves from the paloverde trees and stung Healy's back and neck. But at last the sky in the east began turning faintly gray.

Healy waited until he could see the ground. Then he made a wide circle looking for tracks.

He found absolutely nothing at all. Rain had washed down the hill and into the gully, raising water to a depth of six inches where the horses had stood.

Little rivulets had left their trails straight down the hillside, and although Healy made a circle nearly a mile wide, he found no tracks of any kind.

The Kid was gone, and Nora with him. And Healy would never pick up their trail again. He hesitated for several moments, wondering what was the best thing to do.

He could ride on in the direction the Kid had been traveling but that would be a pure waste of time. The Kid would have changed course just as soon as he was sure rain had wiped out his trail. There was no chance on God's earth of ever picking up the trail.

Arizona Territory comprised thousands of square miles. Nora and the Kid could already be lost in any one of them.

Healy tried to determine, as closely as possible, where he was. Thirty miles east of San Carlos was his closest guess. He would go to San Carlos. There, hard as it would be, he would wait. He would wait for the news of the Apache Kid's latest atrocity. In the meantime he would rest, obtain fresh, strong horses and re-equip himself. With food. With grain for the horses. Maybe Nogal would be there and would agree to help.

When the news came of the Kid's latest attack, he'd be ready. He could ride at top speed to the nearest point where he could cut the Kid's trail. He might even gain an advantage, he thought. He would be rested. The Kid would certainly be tired.

But what about Nora? Could she maintain the pace the Kid would set? He doubted it. He now believed that sooner or later, inevitably, he'd find her dead, the Kid gone, with things done to Nora's body that would make her death ten times more difficult to endure.

He put these thoughts out of his mind, because he knew that kind of thinking would eventually drive him out of his mind. He had to remain cold and sure of himself and he must never let his belief that he would recover Nora alive and unhurt waver or change.

The rain continued to drizzle for a couple of hours before it finally stopped. Healy didn't push his horses very hard for two reasons. One, there wasn't any use. Even if he rode to the Agency at San Carlos at a hard run, he would have to wait hours, maybe days for news of the Kid's latest outrage. Secondly, the footing was dangerous. Horses forced to travel at a pace faster than a walk in the slippery clay underfoot ran the risk of falling and he himself ran the risk of being hurt in the fall.

So he plodded along, soaked to the skin, cold and miserable, but occasionally cursing the Apache Kid bitterly under his breath. He forced himself not to think of Nora, only permitting himself thoughts of the Kid.

He had traveled this country many times with the cavalry, and so knew the landmarks as he knew the back of his hand. He brought the Agency buildings at San Carlos into sight a little before noon and rode straight to the one which housed the Indian Agent's office. He dismounted and tied his saddle horse. He scraped the clay off his feet on the edge of the porch, stamped off what remained and then went inside.

It was a dreary office, with few windows and several benches along the walls. The inner office, that of the Agent, was only slightly larger and slightly lighter. Both offices seemed dreary on this cloudy day.

The Agent had changed since Healy had been gone and so he had to introduce himself. He found the Agent's grip firm and immediately liked the man, whose name was Harvey Cobb. Cobb closed his office door, poured Healy a cup of lukewarm coffee and then sat down behind his desk, prepared to listen to Healy's story all the way from beginning to end.

CHAPTER SEVEN

Healy's first words after their brief introduction were angry ones. 'How the hell did that murderous sonofabitch escape?'

Cobb didn't evade. 'You mean the Apache Kid?'

'That's exactly who I mean.'

'I don't know. I received a routine notification that he had escaped nearly two months ago. I didn't hear anything more and I had about begun to believe he either perished of fever or drowned down there in the swamp.'

'Well, he didn't. I don't know how he did it, but he got back to Arizona and he found out where I'd taken up a ranch. He hit my place two days ago, killed Francisco and María Martínez and stole my wife. I've been after him since then, just about keeping up, until this damned storm hit and I lost his trail.'

'Those aren't your horses, are they? You couldn't have come . . .'

Frank Healy shook his head. 'They belonged to Slattery. But he's got no further need for them. The Kid stabbed him in the back and then killed that Mexican woman who was living with him.'

'And your wife?' Cobb's heavily jowled face was cautiously hopeful.

'She was still alive when the storm wiped out the trail.' He hesitated a moment and then said, 'I don't know if you ever knew her or not. Her maiden name was Corcoran. Mike Corcoran's girl.'

'Didn't know her, but I've heard about her.'

Healy grinned faintly. 'I'll bet you have. Tough as any boy when she was growing up. But oh God, she's going to have to be tougher now than she ever was in her life before.'

There was a silence and then Cobb said, 'I'll send some men to Slattery's to bury him and his woman.' He got up and went outside, short and squat by comparison with Healy, but powerful through the shoulders and narrow in the hips.

Healy was beginning to feel comfortable for the first time, beginning to warm up despite his soggy clothes. There was a telegraph here somewhere, and he was counting on that to bring him news of the Apache Kid's latest raid. In the meantime all he could do was rest, get together an outfit and be ready to go on an instant's notice, night or day.

Cobb was gone only a short time. When he came back, he asked, 'Do you want any of the Apache scouts you rode with before?'

Healy hesitated now. He knew if he took any of the scouts and they failed to get the Kid, he'd revenge himself against them and their families. On the other hand, he sure as hell needed help. He really wanted Nogal, the steadiest, the best tracker of the lot. Besides that, Nogal was a close personal friend and he was nearly as bitterly hated by the Apache Kid as was Healy himself. The Kid blamed Healy and Nogal, more than any of the others, for his capture and subsequent imprisonment.

Healy nodded. 'Just one. Nogal. The Kid hates him as bad as he hates me and when he's finished with me, if I don't get him, he'll be coming after Nogal and his family anyway. I'll ask Nogal if it's all right with you.'

'Sure. Go ahead. Come on. I'll show you where you can stay while you're here. And I'll post a notice in the telegraph office that news of any unexplained killings that come over the wire are to be reported immediately to you.'

Healy said, 'Or horse thefts, or burnings. Anything unusual that would happen to get on the wire.'

Cobb nodded. He led Healy out, along the gallery for about a hundred feet. He opened a door that led to a small room containing a bed, a leather-covered chair and a writing desk and straight-backed chair. He said, 'I'll send for Nogal.'

Healy nodded. Cobb left and Healy walked back to where he'd left his horses. He led them to the room Cobb had assigned him, unsaddled and carried both riding saddle and packsaddle and panniers inside.

He was nervous and jumpy. He tried to sit in the chair and relax but he could not. Finally he unpacked the panniers, then carried all his gear back out on the gallery to dry.

He was making a list of things he would need when he suddenly sensed someone standing in the open door. He glanced up.

It was Nogal, short, sturdy, a little bowlegged, wearing seemingly the same clothing he had worn last time Healy had seen him. His face was slightly flat, his lips narrow, his mouth long. His eyes, which could be as cold and merciless as could those of the Apache Kid, were warm now with pleasure.

Healy crossed the room and shook his hand. He drew Nogal into the room. The Apache scorned both chairs and squatted on his heels with his back against the wall.

Healy said bluntly, 'The Apache Kid has Nora. He hit our place two days ago, killed Francisco and María and took Nora.'

Nogal said, 'If he still have her then he not mean to kill her right away.'

'No. But this damn storm wiped out the trail. Now I've got to wait until he hits someplace else and I hear about it.'

Nogal said, 'That is not all bad. He will take time to rest and your wife be able to rest then too.'

There was a moment's silence between them. Finally Nogal said, 'I go with you.'

That was what Healy had wanted to hear, but he said, 'You know he hates you as much as he hates me. If he rides anywhere close to this place he'll take time to kill your wife and son.'

'I hide them. I take them back into the hills until we catch the Kid.'

Healy asked, 'You're sure this is what you want?'

'I do it partly for you. But I do it for myself and for my family too. If you no get him, he come after me. Besides me, he try to kill my wife and son.'

Healy nodded. 'All right. Get going. Get back as soon as you can because there's no telling when something will come over the telegraph wires.'

Nogal got easily to his feet. He left the room and trotted across the bare space in front of the cluster of Agency buildings toward the wickiups of the Apaches who lived here at the San Carlos Reservation.

Healy led his two horses to the livery stable. There was a large corral out back which contained close to forty head of horses. A tall, bony man with a wide mustache was sitting just inside the door out of the fine drizzle that had begun falling again. He had his chair tilted against the wall, his bootheels hooked over the chair's bottom rung. Healy knew him from Fort Chiricahua, where he had been the sutler for a while about five years back.

Healy stuck out his hand. 'Howdy, Slim. Didn't expect to find you here.'

'Nor me you, Frank. Thought you was ranchin' over in New Mexico.'

'Was. That goddamn Apache Kid got loose

in Florida and came back. Hit my place and killed the couple that worked for me. Stole my wife. I chased him until this storm wiped out the trail. Now I got to wait until he hits someplace else and the news comes over the wire. I'll need a new outfit. I want three of the best horses you got.'

'You gonna trade them two?'

'No. They belonged to Slattery. I never paid for them so they don't belong to me. Guess you can hold 'em until somebody shows up to claim Slattery's Ranch.'

Slim got up and followed Healy out into the corral. He let out a yell that got the horses to running around the corral in a counterclockwise direction. Healy watched the horses carefully and Slim watched Healy.

Frank Healy knew if he made the right choices, Slim would approve. If there was a better horse than one Frank chose, Slim would tell him, because Slim like everybody—man, woman and child—living in Arizona Territory hated the Apache Kid.

Healy said, 'That bay with the blazed face and the two front stockings.'

Slim grunted.

Healy watched some more. After a couple more rounds he said, 'That short-legged steel gray.'

Again Slim grunted. Healy watched the horses running, their hoofs throwing up gobs of mud while Slim kept them moving by an occasional yell or wave of his arms. Finally Healy said, 'That big long-legged sorrel.'

'Why him?' Now Slim's voice was critical.

'To run at the end of the string. Barebacked, he won't tire as fast as a horse with shorter legs.'

Slim nodded approval. Healy said, 'Make me a price. You'll never get 'em back.'

'Two eighty for the three. I'd charge anybody else at least fifty more, but I hate that goddamn Kid as much as anyone. If you can kill him I'll give you the two eighty back.'

Healy dug out his leather money pouch and paid for the horses in gold. Then he took down a rope from the fence and, shaking out a loop, caught the steel gray. He walked along the rope, coiling it. The gray was trembling and he stroked his neck and spoke soothingly to him. He looked at the horse's teeth, then at his hoofs, one by one. To Slim he said, 'Have him shod.'

Slim nodded. Healy caught the other two horses in similar fashion. The bay needed shoeing, but the long-legged sorrel had recently been shod. Healy said, 'Get it done today, will you? There's no telling when I'll get word about where the Kid's hit last.'

'They'll be ready by late this afternoon.'

'I'll want some grain in one of my panniers.'

'Help yourself.' Slim indicated where the grain was kept.

He went next to the Agency store, where he

bought the supplies he thought he and Nogal would need. Nogal would bring his own horse and perhaps a spare, but no pack and no provisions except for some dried jerky.

He didn't know where Nogal would take his family and he didn't care. Just so it was a safe and isolated place that nobody else knew about and just so Nogal didn't leave a plain trail leading there. He cocked an eye at the sky, wondering how much longer the rain was going to last. It was raining harder now—but not hard enough to wash out the trail Nogal and his family made.

He knew Nogal well enough to be sure he wouldn't use horses. They'd go on foot, stepping carefully from rock to rock or from grass clump to grass clump, and Nogal would return the same way, but by a different route.

Slim fired up the forge in the shed behind his livery stable and Healy, having nothing better to do, went back there to help him shoe the two horses. He'd always liked watching a good farrier work—he was only an indifferent one himself, and Slim was good. When a shoe was on and the nails clinched and filed smooth, you couldn't have slipped a piece of paper between shoe and hoof. Slim hummed tunelessly all the time he worked.

In midafternoon the drizzle stopped, the clouds thinned and blue sky showed through. Sun laid a spotted pattern across the steaming land, and by five o'clock most of the clouds had disappeared and it was not only hot but extremely humid too.

Nogal returned. 'They are safe, and they will stay where I have left them until I come for them.'

Healy didn't ask where they were. He didn't want to know. There was always the chance the Kid would capture him and the Kid had ways of making even the strongest of men tell everything they knew. He did, however, ask, 'Manage to cover your tracks pretty good?'

Now a touch of uncertainty touched Nogal's usually inscrutable face and Healy knew he had not covered his tracks. Not well enough so that they could not be picked up by the Apache Kid.

But he would have to find them first, and in a well-populated reservation like San Carlos, the tracks of the people who lived there spread out over an area of a dozen or so square miles. The only trouble was, the rainstorm had wiped out most of the old tracks, leaving the ground as clean as a fresh sheet of writing paper.

Well anyway, the Kid wasn't going to get a chance at trailing Nogal's family. They were going to get him first, and kill him.

The horses were shod, supplies were in the panniers. They could be riding within five minutes of receiving something from the telegrapher telling them where to ride. At five-thirty, Healy and Nogal found the telegraph office, read the notice Cobb had posted on the wall and talked briefly with the telegrapher, an elderly man with mustache and beard and a green eyeshade on his forehead. He said, 'Nothin' yet, boys, but I'll sure as hell get word to you the minute that there is. I get relieved at ten, but I'll tell my relief. You want the word no matter what time of night it comes?'

'No matter what time,' Healy said.

They left, and by smell found the Agency employees' dining room. They went in, got a platter each and went through the line. Healy realized how little he'd had to eat since Nora had been kidnapped, and ate ravenously. Nogal ate sparingly, as he always had since Healy had known him. Afterward they went outside. Both squatted against the wall and rolled cigarettes from Healy's sack.

Healy knew news of the Apache Kid's latest atrocity would not be long in coming. Perhaps tonight. Certainly by morning. He hoped it would not be too impossibly far away. If it wasn't, and if the news came sometime during the night, it was possible they could reach the place as soon as it was light enough to trail.

CHAPTER EIGHT

Nora was as bitterly disappointed as her husband was when the Kid came racing toward her after his confrontation with Frank. He was unhurt. Before the Kid reached her, she saw

Frank appear briefly on the ridge-top behind. He fired at the Kid once, but the range was too great and he wasted neither his time nor ammunition trying further to hit a target that was well beyond the effective range of his gun.

She could guess why Frank had failed to kill the Kid back there on the other side of the ridge. The Kid hadn't been trying to kill Frank so it had not been a duel between the two. He had been trying to kill her husband's horses and thus leave him out here afoot. The frustration of that would have driven Frank nearly out of his mind, and would have been almost harder on him than getting shot.

The Kid reached her, untied her horse and then whacked him savagely across the rump with the barrel of his gun. The horse jumped and broke into a run. In less than a minute they had dropped below a knoll and the ridge where Frank had so briefly appeared was no longer visible to her.

Out of a miserable situation, there were only two things that gave her hope. The Kid was not only angry. He was in a hurry and that meant he had not succeeded in killing Frank's horses. At least not all of them.

She said nothing and made a special effort to keep up, knowing this was not the time to cross the Kid in any way.

Light faded from the sky. Dusk came and went and the sky turned completely black. A low rumble rolled across the land, and glancing in the direction from which it had come, Nora saw a muted flash of lightning, so often called heat lightning, in the distance behind the oncoming clouds. And suddenly the feeling of hope engendered by the Kid's failure to put Frank afoot disappeared. It was going to rain. It seldom rained in this part of the Territory, but it was going to rain tonight. And by morning the trail they had made would be wiped out. Frank would have nothing to follow. He would have lost.

Almost immediately she could see the error of that conclusion. To evade Frank Healy was not the Apache Kid's purpose. He didn't want Frank to lose the trail, at least not permanently.

So the chase was not over. It had hardly begun. But as tired and as sore as she was, Nora knew she'd be grateful for any rest, however short it was going to be. She was as aware as her husband was that one of the most crucial elements that would decide the eventual outcome of this chase was her strength and ability to keep up.

The wind picked up and the air grew chill. Lightning came closer and the thunder became an almost continuous rumble, now deafening, now muted by distance, but by its continuous nature telling her of the storm's magnitude. The storm front was probably at least fifty or sixty miles wide. It would thoroughly soak an area a hundred and fifty miles long. What did it matter that three days from now you wouldn't even be able to tell that it had rained? What mattered was that the trail would be gone. Frank would have to start over, at a disadvantage because the Kid and she would be another sixty to a hundred miles away.

The rain struck, a few great, widely scattered drops at first, then a veritable deluge that soaked Nora to the skin in a couple of minutes, that filled the little gullies and dry arroyos in ten. Their horses waded through a swift-flowing flood that came to their bellies, and floundered in the wet clay on the far bank climbing out.

The Kid occasionally looked back now, as if fearing Nora might try to get away. Finally, considering this a real possibility, he stopped and when her horse caught up, took the reins from her and afterward held onto them.

Nora wondered if she should have tried to get away. She decided it would have been a foolish and unnecessary chance. She was no match for the Apache Kid, even in a rainstorm where visibility was almost negligible and trailing impossible. A foolish and unnecessary chance.

The horses slipped and slid along, sometimes nearly falling, so slippery was the ground underfoot. The Kid rode hunched forward a little, stoically enduring the discomfort of the storm. Nora herself, now thoroughly wet, had given up trying to protect herself from the driving rain or the now cold wind. She shivered miserably, wondering which was worse, the awful heat that robbed her of her strength, or this drenching cold that made her teeth chatter helplessly.

The storm had come upon them from the east. The wind, now, was coming from her left. Unless it had changed direction, which was unlikely, they were going south.

Toward the railroad line between El Paso and Tucson. Toward the stageroad that still was traveled fairly regularly by coaches and freight wagons serving the smaller settlements and ranches lying to north and south of the railroad.

All through the night they rode, until by dawn, Nora was numb with cold and too tired even to shiver anymore. As the sky lightened in the east, she sat and stared numbly at the wide valley that lay before them, at the locomotive smoke and the long line of boxcars and coaches crawling along behind the locomotive toward the west.

The Kid had stopped his horse. Hers stood with his head against the other horse's flank. Both animals were covered with mud. Both were weary beyond belief and stood with their heads hanging listlessly.

The Kid would need fresh horses, Nora thought, but he wasn't going to get them here. Down there the locomotive had stopped beside a tall wooden water tank and was taking on water, while men who looked like ants in the distance loaded lengths of mesquite and ironwood from a huge pile into the tender directly behind the locomotive.

But there were no corrals down there. Only the tank and a small stationhouse that undoubtedly also contained a telegraph instrument because telegraph lines ran along the railroad track in both directions for as far as the eye could see.

The Kid did not turn his head to look at her. He seemed unaware of her. The locomotive belched a dense cloud of black smoke from its stack, belched another cloud of white steam from the region of the wheels, and slowly began to crawl on west.

The sun came up as they sat there and Nora was desperately grateful for the warmth of its rays against her chilled body. Her horse moved so that his entire side was exposed to the sun. Steam began to rise from his wet and muddy hide.

It took nearly half an hour for the train to move down the valley to a distance the Kid apparently considered safe. When it had, he moved on ahead, after handing Nora back the reins of her horse. There was no chance now of her escaping him.

No longer could she see signs of life at the station up ahead. Except for a thin plume of bluish smoke that rose from the tin chimney into the chilly morning air.

The Kid rode about half the distance to the

station before he stopped. He said curtly, 'Get down.'

Nora obeyed instantly. It was good to feel the ground beneath her feet, good to be able to move her arms and legs. But the pleasure was short-lived. The Kid motioned for her to lie down on a rocky spot that was not as muddy as most places were. She knew he was going to tie her hands and feet until after he had finished his grisly business at the isolated railroad depot.

But she obeyed without an argument, which would have been as useless as trying to escape. Swiftly the Kid tied her ankles and her wrists, although not quite as tight as he had previously. She supposed because the leather thongs were wet, and would shrink as they dried.

He tied her horse and his own in a gulch which still had a couple of inches of muddy water running in its bottom, then headed for the railroad station afoot, moving like a shadow from saguaro to mesquite bush, to a pile of rock or a cholla bush. His caution was probably unnecessary because it was likely that the station agent and telegrapher were busy brewing coffee and huddling around the stove.

She lost sight of him before he had gone a hundred yards. And now she waited, appalled at the thought that certain death, in the form of the Kid, was inexorably approaching the station. The men who were going to die had no inkling of his approach. At least, she thought, their deaths would be quick and probably as painless as death can be.

The reason for their death appalled her even more. They were going to die so that word would go out over the telegraph that the Kid had struck again. Right here.

She had the sudden, hopeful thought that the Kid would defeat himself if he killed everybody at the station. He would have to leave one alive to send the message out. But even that hope died as soon as it was born. The Apache Kid was an expert in killing and he could mortally wound a man in such a way that the man would remain conscious and able to get a message out before he died.

Oh God, how she hated him! How she longed for the day when Frank would finally catch up with them, when he could engage the Kid on fair and equal terms! Yet deep inside she knew the terms would never be fair or equal. Not with the Apache Kid. He would rig the final showdown so that only he had a chance of leaving the place alive.

* * *

Jake Kanner was the agent at the station, which bore signs facing both east and west proclaiming that this was Foley, Arizona Territory. Dave Koch was the telegrapher. The telegraph instrument clacked occasionally as the two men stood close to the stove and sipped black coffee brewed in the gray graniteware pot that sat on the top of it.

Koch monitored the messages coming and going over the line absently, knowing how unlikely it was that any one of them would ever be for him but aware enough to pick it up in case one was.

No other train was due for at least ten hours, this one being a late afternoon eastbound headed for El Paso out of Tucson.

Between sips from his steaming cup, Koch said, 'Some storm last night. It's a wonder it didn't blow the wires down.'

'Weren't that much wind. Just rain. We don't need to worry about that water tank being full for a while.' The water tank was filled by a windmill but occasionally during dry periods the groundwater level dropped below the windmill's intake pipe.

The door slammed open with a suddenness and violence that took both men by surprise. Kanner dropped his cup when he saw the Indian, knife in hand, rushing across the tiny room.

The Kid went unerringly to Kanner first, recognizing him as the agent because Koch wore the green eye-shade that was the trademark of a telegrapher. The knife sank deep, straight into Kanner's heart. It was withdrawn instantly, followed by a gush of blood. The Kid avoided Kanner's falling body and came at Koch.

Koch threw his cup of coffee straight into

the Indian's face and turned, heading for the old shotgun that stood in one corner of the cubbyhole that held the telegraph instrument and all the other paraphernalia associated with its use. He never made it. The Kid's knife stabbed deep into his abdomen, a wound the Kid miscalculated because of his anger at being scalded by Koch's coffee. It was a mortal wound, even though death might not come to Koch for an hour or more.

But Koch was not of the stern stuff of which the Kid was made. He felt the excruciating pain, realized he was mortally wounded and promptly lost consciousness.

For an instant the Kid stood there looking down at him, anger and frustration on his face. He had not meant for this one to lose consciousness. He had wanted a message sent from here, that the Apache Kid was on the loose and that he had just struck in this isolated place.

Now the message would not be sent. Not until the late afternoon train for El Paso came in would the word go out over the wires and reach San Carlos, where Frank Healy waited, ready to go, for news.

CHAPTER NINE

The El Paso train pulled in at dusk. The engine stopped beside the water tower to take on water, and the tender crew immediately began loading wood from the pile beside the water tank.

No light showed in the station and the telegraph office was equally dark. The conductor, a grizzled veteran of many years of railroading, curiously left the train and went into the station. Before he could light a match, he stumbled over the body of Jake Kanner. Immediately he struck a match, crossed to the desk and lighted the lamp.

Kanner, stabbed in the heart, had bled profusely at first, but the narrow knife wound had quickly closed and his clothing had absorbed most of the blood. The conductor, whose name was Julius Carnes, went into the cubbyhole reserved for the telegrapher and discovered the body of Dave Koch. Koch had recovered consciousness once, and had tried to crawl to his instrument. He had gotten only as far as the high stool he usually sat upon, but had been unable to climb up its rungs and reach his key.

Carnes breathed, 'Jesus Christ!' in a tone that was more reverent than blasphemous, and hurried out to the train. He told the engineer what had happened, but avoided shouting because he did not want to alarm either the passengers or the crew working at taking on water and loading wood.

The engineer came down and the two men went into the station. The engineer asked,

'What the hell should we do?'

'Do you know how to use a telegraph?'

'A little.'

'Enough to put this on the wires?'

'I'll try.' As he spoke, the instrument clacked briefly and then was silent again. The engineer, Jason Haeger, sat down on the high stool and began to work the key hesitantly. He paused a moment and the instrument clacked back at him almost angrily, certainly with impatience. He worked the key some more. This time, the answering clacking was slow and seemed, by contrast to his earlier reply, patient. He worked for about ten minutes, sometimes pausing for half a minute or so while he tried to remember a certain letter. Finally he stood up and said, 'It's done.'

'Did they say what we should do with the bodies?'

'They said we should put 'em in the baggage car and bring 'em to El Paso with us.'

The conductor went out and opened the door to the baggage car. The wood loading was finished now and they had all the water they needed so the engineer called some of the workmen to carry the bodies out and put them in the baggage car. The workmen did so fearfully, staring with frightened eyes into the darkness beyond the station and the water tank. The baggage door closed and the conductor returned to the station and blew out the lamp. He came out, closing the station door. He climbed aboard the train and it pulled out, gradually picking up speed on the downgrade from this high plain, so near the Continental Divide.

* * *

At the Agency at San Carlos, the message was received, in relayed form, at about eight o'clock. The telegrapher took time to write it swiftly down and then left immediately, heading for the quarters that had been assigned to Frank Healy earlier in the day.

Healy, sitting on the gallery in the evening's cool, saw him coming. He snatched the yellow telegram form and read it hastily using the small amount of light coming from a lamp inside the room. He handed the form back, then, running, headed for the corral behind the livery barn.

Slim was still there, also enjoying the evening's cool. Frank said, 'Grab a horse and go get Nogal, will you? We've got a trail.'

He could see that Slim wanted to ask questions but the stableman threw a bridle on a horse and leaped astride barebacked. He thundered toward the Indian wickiups.

Frank Healy caught his three horses and led them along the gallery to the room Cobb had given him. His gear was nearly dry by now. He was careful that both his saddle blanket and the pad that went under the packsaddle went on smooth, then he put on the saddles and cinched them down. He brought out the panniers and hung them from the packsaddle, having already filled one side with oats, the other with provisions and supplies. He lashed them down.

Nogal arrived, riding one horse, leading two others. Slim was with him. He said, 'Before you leave, tell me what happened.'

Healy figured he owed Slim that. He said, 'The Kid hit the railroad station at Foley forty miles south of here early this morning. Killed the agent and the telegrapher. He gut-stabbed the telegrapher, figuring he'd get a message out. But the guy died and word of what happened had to wait on the El Paso train.'

He tied the long-legged sorrel to the tail of the bay, on which he had put the packsaddle. Then he mounted the gray and without speaking again rode out, taking the road that headed south out of the San Carlos Agency. Nogal fell in silently behind.

In a way it was encouraging to know that the Apache Kid sometimes made mistakes. He had made one when he stabbed the telegrapher in a vital area. Healy was sure the Kid had not wanted him to wait this long for news of the attack.

But he had been forced to wait because the telegrapher had died without getting the message out. And now the Kid was probably an extra fifty or sixty miles ahead.

They could reach the railroad station tonight. They'd even have to wait for it to get light enough to trail. But the Kid would have by then a twenty-four-hour lead.

Healy felt sure that was more lead than he wanted. But maybe he'd make another mistake. They might even get lucky enough to cross his trail close behind him as he crisscrossed back again from wherever he had gone.

Frank Healy paced his saddle horse carefully. Even if they reached the railroad station at Foley in the middle of the night, it wasn't going to do them any good. Even Nogal couldn't follow trail in the dark.

They'd be better off saving their horses' strength and trying to reach Foley a little before dawn. Then, as soon as it was light, they could be off again on the trail of the Apache Kid.

Healy knew where Foley was. He also knew that about ten miles west of it and a mile or so north, there was a ranch, Kreisler's. The Kid would by now have attacked that too, with more purpose this time since he would need fresh horses by the time he got to it.

The night hours passed. Healy thought of Nora and wondered how she was holding up. The storm would have thoroughly soaked and chilled her and she would have been bitterly cold all through the night. He felt his eyes begin to burn and shook his head angrily.

Toughness was needed now, not sentiment. There'd be time for that later, after unyielding toughness had rescued her.

Once, when Nogal ranged up alongside Healy asked, 'How's your wife and boy? I'll bet the kid is getting pretty big.'

'Sure. He get big. How come you no kids?'

Healy grinned. 'It's not because I haven't tried.'

That made him think of holding Nora in the night and the grin faded from his face. 'Did you get them stashed away in a fairly safe place?'

The scout grunted his yes.

Healy could detect a note of worry in the sound. He said, reassuringly, 'He won't go after them until he's killed me. I'm first on his list. Only he's not going to kill me. I'm going to get him instead.'

They lapsed into silence again and Nogal fell back until he was riding almost a hundred yards behind. Healy was thinking that the Kid's attack on the railroad station had not been aimless. He had killed the two men for the sole purpose of seeing to it Healy got word of his whereabouts.

Healy didn't even want to count the men and women the Kid had killed since the first attack on his ranch. Anymore than he wanted to count those the Kid had killed before they caught him and sent him to Florida. He could guess that the Kid's habits hadn't changed any on his way back to Arizona Territory from Florida. The strange thing was that no word of any unexplained killings had reached the Territory and been reported in the newspapers.

At about one in the morning, they reached the wide flat where the railroad tracks were. They came to the stageroad and turned into it, since traveling the road was easier on the horses than following the tracks. After riding about five miles, Healy spotted the dark bulk of the water tower half a mile south of the road, and headed toward it.

They reached the station and tied the horses to the legs of the water tower. Healy went into the station and lighted the lamp. The telegraph instrument clacked intermittently.

There was a little blood on the floor of the station, quite a lot of it in beside the telegrapher's stool. It was smeared here, as if the man had tried to drag himself from where he was stabbed to his instrument. He obviously hadn't made it, or Healy and Nogal would have gotten the news of this attack yesterday morning instead of after dark last night.

Two men, doing their jobs, harming no one and completely unused to violence. The Kid had struck like a rattlesnake, deadly and unexpected, and it had probably been all over in less than a minute, too soon for either man to realize what was happening.

He thought back to the little ambush the Kid had laid for him so that he could kill his horses and leave him afoot. He went over it again and again in his mind, trying to figure out what he might have done differently.

But there wasn't anything. He'd known the Kid wanted to kill his horses and leave him afoot and he'd concentrated on saving them, which had given the Kid time to get away.

But what if he'd gone single-mindedly after the Kid, and concentrated on killing him instead of worrying about whether the Kid killed his horses or not. Well, that might have worked. He might have succeeded in killing the Kid. Yet, knowing how the Kid could disappear in brush or cactus clumps or low piles of rock, he knew he might also have missed while the Kid did not.

And besides, he'd only had seconds to decide what he should do. He hadn't been able to weigh alternatives.

He looked at Nogal. 'We could ride down to Kreisler's. It's a lead pipe cinch he went there from here. He'd have to have horses and he sure didn't get any of them here.'

Nogal nodded. The two men went outside and headed for the water tank where the horses were tied. From down the track toward the west came the faint, mournful sound of a train whistle. Healy said, 'What the hell? There isn't supposed to be an eastbound at this time of night.'

They waited. The train's headlight became visible, an orange spot that glowed in the darkness as the train rattled along the track.

Their horses, unused to trains, plunged and a couple of them bucked as the train pulled into the station. The engine stopped beside the water tank, which positioned the cars in front of the station and its small platform.

Steam hissed from the drive wheels. Healy stared down the line of cars, a slight frown of puzzlement on his brow. Nothing but boxcars, all with their doors closed.

A couple of men began taking on water from the tank. A couple more went into the station and lighted lamps, plainly a replacement station manager and telegrapher. Others went down the line of closed boxcars, opening their doors.

From out of the first one so opened leaped a horse with a cavalryman on his back. Another followed and another, and as each boxcar was opened up, more cavalrymen leaped their horses to the ground. One fell, and broke a leg, and after a lot of talk and bitter, angry cursing, a single shot rang out.

Healy and Nogal stood on the small station platform in the glow of light now coming through the windows and open door. A man rode to the platform, dismounted and stepped up on it.

Both Healy and Nogal recognized him immediately. He was Lieutenant Angus MacBrayer from Fort Chiricahua, but how he happened to be here was something Healy could not understand.

The three men were friends of long standing, and they shook hands enthusiastically all around. Healy asked finally, 'How the hell did you get here so fast?'

'We were in Tucson. When they got the news of what the Kid did here, they made up a special train an' put us on it. Now, by God, they expect us to run him down. You have orders to scout for us. You and Nogal.'

Healy shook his head. 'Huh uh. Not a chance. Nogal's an Indian and I'm a civilian. We're not subject to orders.'

'Frank . . .' MacBrayer knew he didn't have a chance of getting closer than fifty miles to the Apache Kid without Healy's and Nogal's help. But he had his orders too.

Frank said, 'The best you can do is station two or three men at each of the ranches within a fifty-mile radius of here. And maybe keep moving with the men you've got left. You got Sergeant Mallory and he can follow trail damn near as well as I can. Take him down the track to Kreisler's. That's where the Kid would have had to go for fresh horses, and that's where we're going to pick up the trail as soon as it's light enough.'

MacBrayer looked disappointed in the light coming from the lamps inside the station. Out in the darkness his men milled around, their non-coms yelling, trying to get them ready to ride as soon as it was light.

But MacBrayer knew as well as Healy did

that trying to catch the Kid with a troop of cavalry was a foolish, impossible task. He said, 'If we can help you in any way—supplies, horses—you'll let me know, won't you?'

Healy nodded. He and Nogal were ready and there was a line of gray silhouetting the horizon in the east. By the time they reached Kreisler's, it would be light enough to trail.

CHAPTER TEN

Lieutenant MacBrayer watched Healy and Nogal disappear into the growing light of dawn. The train crew had finished taking on water and loading the tender with wood and were ready to pull out. They would go on to Mesilla, and would probably remain there on a siding for a day or two until the railroad authorities decided what to do with them.

In the meantime, he was stuck here with his troop, small as it was, consisting of only thirty-six men besides himself. He didn't have enough men to send out patrols and he knew, if his superiors did not, that trying to follow the Apache Kid with a troop of cavalry was a classic waste of time.

Healy's suggestion was probably the best, he thought. He called for Sergeant Mallory and the two went into the station, while the men lounged on the platform, smoking and talking but throwing an occasional sharp glance out across the flat in case the Apache Kid was still lurking there.

MacBrayer said, 'All right, Sergeant, you know this country a lot better than I do. Where are the places, within fifty or sixty miles, where the Apache Kid can get fresh horses and supplies?'

Mallory dug a stub of pencil from his pocket, then got up and went into the telegrapher's cubbyhole, where he tore off a message blank. He came back, drew a long line across the sheet and put an X in the middle of it. 'The line's the railroad, sir, and the X is where we are.' With his forehead slightly furrowed, he located one by one the places he could remember as potential sources for fresh horses. There were Kreisler's and Slattery's and the San Carlos Agency. But there were others. South of the railroad there were Haley's Wells, Jacoby's Ranch and the tiny settlement of Rincon. North of the tracks, besides Slattery's and the Agency, there were Blackstone's, a roadhouse, saloon and livery stable, and Lawson, a town of perhaps a dozen residents. That was five places the Kid might resupply himself with horses. Mallory said, 'You go beyond that sixty-mile circle, and the Kid might, and there's at least a dozen other places.'

MacBrayer shook his head. 'We can't cover all of them. If we cover the ones within sixty miles and keep a few men here, it's going to be about the best we can do. Detail three men to ride to each of those places except for Slattery's and the Agency. And Kreisler's. He's already hit those places and likely won't bother with them again.'

'Yes sir. That leaves Haley's Wells, Jacoby's and Rincon south of here. And Blackstone's and Lawson to the north. That'll take fifteen men.'

'Then send four to each. That damned Apache Kid can kill three men before they figure out what's going on.'

'Yes sir. Right away.'

'And tell 'em this isn't a damned picnic. The Kid is going to hit every one of those places before he's through.'

'Yes sir. I'll tell 'em sure enough. But . . .'

'Send someone steady with each group. A corporal. Or a private who can make the others do what he tells them to. An old hand.'

'Yes sir.'

'And get them started right away. Do you think they can find those places without getting lost?'

'Can't vouch for that, Lieutenant. But I'll give 'em the best directions I know how to give.'

MacBrayer nodded and the sergeant left. MacBrayer thought that if he sent out twenty men, he'd have sixteen left. Enough to successfully guard this small railroad station and Kreisler's Ranch. And he'd have enough men to go to the assistance of Healy and Nogal, if that assistance should be requested.

Nothing more was likely to happen here, or at Kreisler's, to the west. Healy and Nogal were not going to ask his help. The only possible chance his men had of engaging the Apache Kid would be if the Kid tried raiding one of the places to which MacBrayer had dispatched a four-man detail.

The sad truth was that the Army was no match for these Apache renegades. Their horses were too slow and the only chance they ever got to engage the Apaches in battle was at times the Apaches chose, and in places that favored them.

Relentless pressure by large numbers of United States troops had admittedly forced most of the formerly warlike Apaches onto the reservations.

But without the Apache scouts, renegades like the Apache Kid and Geronimo could roam and raid and kill at will all over the Territory. MacBrayer wished briefly and wistfully that instead of thirty-six troopers he had half a dozen scouts. If he had, he might have had a chance.

* * *

Healy led the way along the track until they were opposite Kreisler's Ranch. Then he swung his horse northward, and as the sun poked above the flat horizon to the east, they rode into Kreisler's yard. The corral was empty, the gate standing open. Healy said, 'Take a look at the tracks. See how many horses he got and what kind they were.'

He rode to the house himself. Right in front of it were two dead horses, their throats cut and pools of blood beneath the wounds. The hide had been skinned back from the hindquarter of one and a piece of meat cut out probably weighing somewhere between five and ten pounds. Healy thought that if the Kid knew how far he was ahead, he might take time to cut the meat into strips and lay it out on mesquite bushes to dry. It wouldn't dry completely in the time he had, but he could keep it from spoiling by partially drying it.

He went on into the house, steeling himself for what he might find. Otto Kreisler lived here with a Papago Indian wife and a couple of small children. He expected to find bodies in the kitchen, but there were none.

He called out, knowing there was no sense in it, then proceeded through the house. He searched the downstairs without finding either bodies or anything amiss. He climbed the stairs, to find the upstairs as empty as the downstairs had been.

Thank God! For once the murderous Kid had been thwarted. There hadn't been anybody here for him to kill.

He went outside. Nogal was coming from the

corral. He said, 'Two horses. That's all in the corral. Kreisler must go to Tucson. Tracks of a team and buckboard head that way.'

'What way did the Kid and Nora go?'

'North. Toward San Carlos.'

Nogal's face might have seemed inscrutable to someone who knew him less well than Healy did. But Healy could see the worry in his eyes. He said, 'He's 'way ahead of us. And he knows it. What do you figure he'll do?'

'Maybe go to San Carlos and try find my family. Maybe find a good place to rest. Who knows what Apache Kid going to do?'

Healy breathed, 'God, I hate that sonofabitch! When we catch him . . .'

Nogal made the faintest of smiles. '*If* we catch him . . .'

'We'll get him. We got him before.'

'We had dozen scouts before.'

Healy studied Nogal's face. 'You got any doubts?'

Nogal didn't answer immediately. Finally he said, 'No doubts. But Apache Kid slippery as snake.'

'What about Nora? What do you think her chances are?'

'If the Kid going to kill her he do it long time ago. If he want to torture her and hurt you that way, he do that long time ago. I don't know what he's got in mind, but if Nora keep up, she stay alive.'

The trail led steadily north until, about five

miles from the railroad line, it turned abruptly around and headed south, on a course that would miss Kreisler's by several miles. Healy asked, 'Now what the hell's he up to?'

'He look for high place where he watch his back trail and where he find feed and water for horses.'

'And where would that place be?'

'Yucca Flats. There a high rim facing north and much good grass. After the rain, water collect in every low place for miles and Jacoby's Ranch less than ten miles away.'

'You're sure that's where he'll go?'

'As sure as can be, about Apache Kid.'

'You think we ought to forget the trail and head for there?'

'You boss, my friend. But if was me, that what I'd do.'

'All right. We'll do it. But we still won't close the gap to more than five or six hours, no matter how hard we ride.'

Nogal shrugged. 'That better than a day and night.'

Now, in spite of the lead the Kid had, Healy began to let himself dream about surprising the Apache resting on Yucca Flats. He knew it was an unlikely chance, but it was a possibility. He spurred his horse and belabored his rump with the rifle barrel until the horse was running. He held this pace as long as he dared before letting the horse slow to a lope. Nogal made no effort to keep the gap between them closed, but let his horses lag until he was nearly a quarter mile behind.

Healy grinned faintly to himself, thinking of the difference between white men and Indians. White men, even those in a hurry, would nearly always ride abreast whenever the terrain permitted, so that they could talk. Indians rode single file, too widely separated for talk which didn't seem to interest them.

It was still fairly early when they crossed the road and then the railroad tracks and, riding hard, headed south toward Mexico. Once, when he stopped briefly to rest the horses, Healy asked of Nogal, 'Do you think he could be headed into Mexico? The Sierra Madre?'

Nogal considered that only briefly. Then he shook his head. 'The Kid not really want to get away. He want to wear us out and put you through hell worrying about your wife. If he finds out I'm with you, he going to head for San Carlos to try to find my wife and boy.'

'Maybe he won't find out.'

Nogal smiled faintly. 'He find out all right. He make it a point to cross our back trail and then he know someone is with you. And he know it is me.'

Another thought occurred to Healy. 'What if heading south was just a ruse? What if he's really headed for San Carlos now?'

He could see that worried Nogal. The Apache considered it for several moments and finally he said, 'It could be a trick. Let's split.

You go left and I go right.' He pointed ahead at a cone-shaped hill perhaps fifteen miles away. He said, 'We can meet there. If neither of us has found his trail, then we better turn around and head for San Carlos again.'

He swung his horses left, maintaining the same steady gallop, and Nogal swung right. Healy kept his eyes on the ground, only glancing up occasionally to check the land around him, making sure there was nothing that could hide the Kid, his horses and Nora and make possible an ambush. Not that there was much chance of it. He was following no trail. There was no reason for the Kid to expect him to be in this particular place, following this particular route.

He cut the Kid's trail before he had gone more than half a dozen miles. He withdrew the Spencer from its boot, pointed it in the general direction Nogal had taken, and fired it. Then he dismounted, taking advantage of this necessary wait to rest his mounts.

While he was waiting, he studied the tracks. The Kid had been riding in the lead, on a very fine horse he had stolen at Kreisler's. Healy could tell the horse's quality to a large extent by the shape and size of his hoofs and by the way he ran.

Nora's horse appeared to be behind the Kid's horse by thirty or forty feet. He studied the hoofprints of Nora's horse. This one had not the strength or quality of the horse the Kid had stolen, but he seemed to be keeping up. At least for now.

He saw Nogal coming at a lope about half a mile away. Without even seeing the Apache's face, he knew how relieved he would be. The Apache Kid was not yet ready to head for San Carlos. Probably he did not yet know Nogal was with Healy on his trail. He had indeed been heading for Yucca Flats, and perhaps ten or twelve hours' rest for himself and Nora. He knew Jacoby's Ranch was close and that fresh horses would be available to him there.

MacBrayer had dispatched men to Jacoby's, as well as to all the other places the Kid could supply himself, at least those within fifty or sixty miles. But the troopers would not arrive until after the Kid had hit the place and gone. He was at least fifteen hours ahead right now, according to the tracks. Yucca Flats was two or three hours away. If he had traveled three hours and rested ten, he had already hit Jacoby's Ranch. The troopers would arrive in time to bury Jacoby's body, that of his wife, and those of his children, a girl of about twelve and a boy of seven.

Nogal arrived. Healy said, 'He's heading south, all right. But he's maybe fifteen hours ahead. Which means he's already taken his rest at Yucca Flats and that he's already hit Jacoby's Ranch.

'Then let's head for Jacoby's.' There was a sympathetic yet wary look in Nogal's eyes as he spoke. Healy had traveled with him enough and known him long enough to know exactly what he was thinking. If the Kid had had a ten-to-twelve-hour rest at Yucca Flats, he would most certainly have forced Nora and the sign of the struggle would be there on the ground for him to read. By persuading him to go straight to Jacoby's, Nogal was trying to spare him that sight.

Healy told himself he didn't care. He loved Nora; she was his wife. And he would have been the last to want her to resist the Kid because doing so would mean certain death. And yet he did care. His stomach turned at the thought. 'Goddam sonofabitch.'

Jacoby's was maybe a couple of hours away, three if they risked everything and ran the horses, expecting to get more at Jacoby's Ranch. But the Kid had most likely taken what horses were at Jacoby's.

Healy slowed his horse and let Nogal catch up. He said, 'He was fifteen hours ahead of us. If he took twelve to rest at Yucca Flats, and then went to Jacoby's for horses, it means he's only a couple of hours ahead of us. Let's do a little figuring. Where do you think he'd go from Jacoby's?'

Shaking his head Nogal said, 'He maybe not yet be at Jacoby's. He no need fresh horses yet. But maybe soon. I think we separate. I follow trail to Yucca Flats. You head for Jacoby's Ranch.'

Healy nodded. He then turned a little toward the east and headed straight for Jacoby's at a lope. Nogal took the Apache Kid's trail and headed toward Yucca Flats at the same hard pace. If there was evidence there that Nora had been raped, at least Healy would not have to see it. He would be at Jacoby's Ranch.

CHAPTER ELEVEN

After he had finished at the railroad station, the Apache Kid made it back to where he had left Nora so silently that he startled her when he suddenly appeared a dozen yards away. He knelt and swiftly untied the leather thongs. Then he went after the horses while Nora rubbed her wrists and walked back and forth, trying to restore circulation to her legs. Something new was beginning to worry her, something that struck sheer terror into her heart. What if the Kid left her tied too long? Or what if he tied her and then something happened to him and he did not return at all? She would lose her legs and maybe her arms as well, and she knew she would prefer death to that. What kind of wife could she be to Frank with only one leg, or none? Or without both her arms?

So each time she was untied, she worked

frantically to restore circulation to both her arms and legs until she was forced to mount and move on again.

They rode west toward a cluster of buildings barely visible in the distance. While they were still a mile away, the Kid found a place where he could hide the horses, ordered her to dismount and again tied her wrists and ankles.

The first time he had tied her, she had struggled and tried to free herself. Now she knew better. Struggling only made her wrists and ankles sore and she had decided that even if she did get free of the leather thongs, she would still be at the Kid's mercy when he returned. Even taking both horses wouldn't help, since the Kid's purpose each time he left was to secure fresh ones. Except back there at that little railroad station. She might have tried escaping there. He'd have made it on foot to the ranch where he was now, would have obtained fresh horses and taken her trail. He'd have caught her before she'd gone a dozen miles and would almost certainly have killed her for causing him so much trouble by trying to get away.

He returned quickly with fresh horses and with a flour sack filled with provisions. There was no fresh blood on him this time and she decided that no one had been at the ranch when he arrived. He untied her again and she mounted. He led out at his usual pace, a lope which, whenever possible, he speeded up to a steady run. Only when both horses were lathered and winded did he slow to a trot to give them a chance to rest.

He headed directly south and she wondered, fearfully, if he was finally heading into the Sierra Madre in Mexico. He was angry about something. That was obvious to her but she had no idea what his anger was about.

They traveled south for nearly half a day, and then began climbing steadily through dry land covered with giant saguaros. The saguaros thinned as the altitude increased, to be replaced gradually by giant yucca or Joshua trees, and at last they came to a shallow rock rim and, after they had negotiated that, reached the top of a plateau that seemed to stretch away for fifty miles in rolling, shallow, undulating swells.

The Kid halted at the top of the rim, dismounted and motioned for her to do likewise. He tossed the sack of provisions at her and said, 'Build fire. Cook.'

She dismounted with alacrity. There was some scattered cholla cactus in the area and each plant had a dead branch or two which she knew would burn. She walked as quickly as she could, grateful for the chance to move around. She gathered an armload, brought it back to where the Kid had staked out the horses, then went back for another load. By the time she returned with this one, the Kid had a fire going, one that was small and nearly smokeless.

She felt a touch of fear. The Apache Kid was a man with all the drives and desires of one. And she was a woman, unable to protect herself.

Hoping to divert his thoughts, she added sticks to the fire and began to cook the meat he had brought from the last ranch on spits of green ocotillo. She knew Apaches didn't care much for potatoes but there were some in the sack so she placed them carefully in the coals at the edge of the fire to bake, after first coating them with mud. There was a loaf of home-baked bread and she cut off part of it and placed it near the fire to warm.

The sun traveled slowly across the sky and began to sink toward the horizon in the west. Night was the time that Nora feared the most, and what she hoped to accomplish was to feed the Apache Kid so well that he would go to sleep early. Without molesting her.

In late afternoon the meal was ready. The Kid gnawed gingerly on one of the hot spitted pieces of meat, and ate the potato and bread between mouthfuls of meat. Nora also ate, as quickly as she could. She knew she needed above all else to keep up her strength and she could not do that without food.

The Kid finished eating. He whittled a toothpick with his razor-sharp knife, then picked his teeth. Afterward he sharpened the knife on a stone he carried for that purpose.

Nora cleaned up what little mess was left

over from the meal, and burned the ocotillo spits and scraps and potato skins. She left, walking into the darkness, and returned with a load of wood. Again she went out and again and after the fourth load, the Kid said harshly, 'Enough wood. Come here.'

There was sheer terror in her eyes as she looked at him. She stood frozen, unable to move either toward him or away from him.

He got up, like a great, lazy cat. He reached her, seizing her, and bore her to the ground.

Every instinct told her to fight. But her intelligence told her how useless it would be. If she fought, he would force her. If she angered him, he would kill her. However revolting and repugnant what was going to happen would be, it would not bring any harm to her. Fighting would.

When it was over, he rose and looked down at her with contempt. 'Damn poor squaw. Healy fool for following.'

She made no reply. She straightened her clothing, then found herself a place to sleep. The Kid was already lying on the far side of the fire, his eyes closed. Before she had finished settling herself for the night, he was snoring softly.

She felt tears burning in her eyes, running silently across her cheeks. For a while she wept this way and then, despite her determination to control herself, she began to sob. She covered her mouth and nose with her hands so that no sound would escape and wake the Kid.

Hopelessness and depression overcame her. Maybe it would be better if she was dead. Then maybe her husband would stop following. Maybe then he would take her body home and let the proper authorities run down the Apache Kid.

But she knew that wasn't true. If the Kid killed her, Frank would spend the rest of his life if necessary pursuing him, and in the end either Frank or the Kid, or both, would die. No. She would have to go on. She would have to conserve her strength. Maybe, she thought with some bitterness, the Kid considered her such a poor squaw that he wouldn't molest her again.

It surprised her that he hadn't bothered to tie her, but when she turned over once, she saw his eyes come open. As long as she was near him, he didn't need to tie her. He was like a cat, sleeping lightly and coming awake at every tiny noise.

She slept finally, and was roused in late morning by the Kid's moccasin toe digging into her side. He growled, 'Get up, squaw. We go.'

There was a small amount of cooked meat left over from last night. The Kid apparently didn't want it, so she took it herself and as they rode south she chewed it determinedly, but slowly, so that eating it would not increase her thirst.

Now he turned and headed east and Nora breathed a sigh of relief. At least he wasn't heading into Mexico. She had heard enough of the Sierra Madre to know her strength would probably fail in those terrible, trackless mountains. Furthermore, she knew his lead had been cut drastically. He could not, now, be more than a few hours ahead of Frank.

The Kid maintained a steady lope for half the morning, in a direction that was almost exactly east. Gradually, however, the Kid slowed his pace. He slowed to a trot, and then a walk, and then briefly returned to a lope for less than a couple of hundred yards before slowing to a trot again.

He did something else she found strange. He dismounted and, standing on a rock, tied a rope to one of his horse's forefeet. At intervals afterward, he would pull on the rope, causing the horse to stagger, as if from weakness.

Nora began to understand. The Kid knew Frank would be along sometime today. Heading east, he was probably pointing his course for the nearest ranch where fresh horses would be available. But now, he wanted Frank to think his horses were weakening.

She could not understand his strategy, but she knew he had one. The Kid never did anything without a reason. If he wanted Frank to believe his horses were weakening and if he succeeded in making him believe it, then it would further some plan he had for catching Frank off guard.

Some way, she must warn Frank. But there

was no way she could tell him in so many words that the Kid's strategy was false. The best she could do would be to drop an occasional scrap of cloth when the Kid wasn't looking, in a place impossible for the Kid to see. The scraps of cloth would tell Frank she was trying to pass him a message. And even if he didn't know what the message was, he might be more wary and even more on guard. They rode through a jumble of huge rocks surrounded by mesquite.

Stealthily, she tore a scrap from her already tattered petticoat. She waited until some rocks were between the Kid and herself and then dropped it. The breeze caught it and carried it to one side of the trail.

Cautiously, careful that the sound of tearing cloth did not reach the Kid's ears, she detached another scrap of cloth. Once more she dropped it when it seemed there would be no chance of the Kid's seeing it.

She dropped two more scraps of cloth. Finally, fearing she would be discovered, she gave it up. Frank would surely see at least one out of the four, even if a wind came up. He would know she was trying to warn him of something.

They had traveled a couple of hours with the Kid's horse artificially lame, when he suddenly stopped, dismounted and untied the rope he had secured to his horse's forefoot. He remounted and abruptly turned south again, urging both horses into a lope.

Now she understood. The Kid had tried to give Frank the idea that he was heading for a nearby ranch to replace his horses. He had reinforced the idea by making his own horse appear lame. Now he would circle back and lay an ambush for Frank, who would be hurrying even more since he would believe the Kid's horse was lame.

Her eyes seemed to burn a hole in the back of the Apache Kid's head. What quirk of nature caused such monsters to be born? The Kid must have killed forty or fifty people in the course of his life, maybe more. And so far, God had seen fit to let him survive despite the efforts of half a hundred whites in the Territory to take his life.

The Kid, as if feeling the intensity of her glance, turned his head and looked at her. He could not have helped seeing the bitter hatred in her eyes. But it seemed to affect him not at all. He simply turned his head to the front again.

This was the devil, she thought, in human form. Powerful, evil, capable of being defeated only by someone whom God favored and helped. She wondered, for the first time, if Frank was capable of overcoming such evil. Frank had never been a churchgoer. He adhered to no particular religion. So far as she knew, he never prayed, and she wasn't even sure he believed in God. Could such a man defeat the devil all by himself? Could good triumph over evil in this situation? Nora knew as well as anyone that good was not always triumphant. Quite often evil was victorious. She thought, 'Oh God, give him strength. Give him cunning. Give him the ability to understand what my little scraps of cloth meant. Let him rid this territory of this murderous monster who takes human life as lightly as a small boy steps upon a grasshopper.'

And she knew that even if it cost her her life, she would warn Frank when the time for it came. She would not remain silent while the Kid successfully ambushed Frank.

They traveled south at a lope for a couple of miles. Then the Kid turned west and after five or six miles traveling west, turned north again. From this distance, about two miles, she could see the place he had picked to ambush Frank. It was a cluster of huge, rounded rocks piled up upon a hill, and surrounded by mesquite, a phenomenon that often occurs in the broad Southwest. They had passed, a couple of hours ago, right through the rocky pile. Frank would also pass that way.

There was plenty of cover for the horses and a little grass on this side of the hill. The Kid had probably checked the place thoroughly when they rode by it earlier to make sure the cover it provided was adequate.

She'd never get an opportunity to warn Frank, she thought. The Kid would tie her well back in the rocks and would gag her so that she could not cry out.

CHAPTER TWELVE

Healy occasionally glanced back over his shoulder at Nogal, who was loping steadily toward Yucca Flats, the rimrock of which was barely visible in the distant haze. He himself headed east toward Jacoby's Ranch. He didn't know it but the plan they had evolved would save him from the Kid's ambush. It would also prevent him from finding the small, warning scraps of cloth that Nora had dropped for him.

Nogal rode straight south toward the distant rim, until he disappeared, staying with the trail of the Apache Kid. The trail was easy to follow and required only a small part of his attention. He expected no ambush here for at least two reasons. It was fairly level ground, with few places suitable for ambushing anyone. And the trail was nearly twenty-four hours old, all but eliminating any chance the Kid would be waiting for them to come along.

Yet Nogal knew the Kid, and so did not entirely rule out the chance that the Kid would ambush him. The Kid relied as much as possible on surprise. And what could be more surprising than for him to wait twenty-four hours for his prey to ride into his trap.

Nogal reached the shallow sandstone rim

and climbed his horse up through it. He found the Kid's camp almost at its edge, and dismounted so that he could study the signs on foot.

By carefully checking the ground, and the remains of the fire, Nogal was able to tell that the Kid and Nora Healy had spent a night and a good part of a day here. The Kid's two horses, knee-deep in grass and with water aplenty, would have had time to rest and recover their strength. So the Kid didn't need fresh horses immediately.

And that was dangerous because it gave the Kid a freedom of movement he could not enjoy if his horses had to be replaced immediately.

Nogal had figured he would go to Jacoby's eventually. But not just yet. And what he would be doing in the meantime was something Nogal would have to find out.

Nogal finished examining the Kid's campsite, then, assured that he had found everything that had any bearing on the Kid's intentions, he rode away, following the Kid's and Nora's trail.

The trail headed east toward Jacoby's at a lope, and Nogal took it. Both horses the Kid had seemed strong and traveled steadily. Nogal held his horse to an alternating lope and trot, aware his horse had not rested the way the Kid's horses had. Occasionally, he dismounted and studied the tracks of the Kid's horses. The Kid was now maybe two hours ahead of him.

He rode steadily until midmorning. Then, suddenly, he noticed that one of the Kid's horses was lame, the one the Kid was riding since his tracks were often overlaid by those of the horse following.

He pulled aside immediately, dismounted, and walked back to the place where the Kid's horse had first turned lame. He knelt, a couple of feet from the tracks. He found it strange that nothing appeared to have caused the lameness. The horse had not stepped on a sharp rock, or picked up a thorn or otherwise hurt himself.

Nogal continued to squat there patiently, scanning every square inch of the ground. And then he saw a tiny shred of leather on a rock a foot from where he was. And he noticed that the Kid's horse had, for just an instant, lifted the foot that had, moments later, turned up lame.

He knew now what the Kid had done. He had dismounted onto the rock where the shred of leather from his moccasin had been caught, and had lifted the horse's foot long enough to tie a rope or leather thong to his fetlock. Afterward, by keeping a slight pressure on the rope every time the horse was about to put down his foot, he made the animal appear to be lame.

Nogal mounted and took the trail again, his mind racing. The Kid had wanted his horse to appear lame and there could be but one reason for that. He wanted Healy, whom he believed to be his pursuer, to think he was headed for Jacoby's Ranch. And since that was his logical destination anyway, it followed that he did not intend to go to Jacoby's Ranch at all, at least not yet. He had another plan.

Passing through a jumble of huge rocks and mesquite something fluttering along the ground fifteen or twenty feet from the trail caught Nogal's eye. He rode to it, dismounted and picked it up. It was a small fragment of a woman's dress or petticoat, and could belong to no one but Nora Healy. Nor was it possible for it to have been torn loose accidentally. The cactus and brush were too low here.

He went on, more and more cautiously, sure of an ambush now. He found fragments two, three and four, and, a dozen miles farther on, found where, suddenly, the Kid had turned south. He knew there would be an ambush now. He had, due to the Kid's 'lame horse' ruse, passed the place the Kid had picked for it before the Kid arrived to set it up. Knowing which way the trail would turn eventually, Nogal followed it, extremely watchful now. A few miles farther on, he found where it had turned west, and shortly thereafter where it had turned north again.

No longer was the Kid's horse limping. Nogal wasn't given to feeling excitement, but he felt it now. The Kid was ahead of him and he knew what the Kid intended to do. All he had to do was follow this trail and stay alert.

With a little luck he could turn the tables and take the Kid from behind. But he promised himself there would be no attempt to take the Kid alive. He would kill him like a scorpion, with no more hesitation and certainly with no regret.

* * *

Healy took a straight cross-country route from where he left Nogal toward Jacoby's Ranch. It was the only place for fifty miles where the Kid could get fresh horses, and it was logical that the kid would head for it sooner or later.

Maybe he didn't need fresh horses now. But he would before he reached another place he could get them. He had to go to Jacoby's eventually. He had to.

And yet, a vague uneasiness began to fester in his brain because he knew how sly the Kid was and he also knew that the Kid never went after fresh horses until the ones he had were completely worn out.

No, he finally decided, the Kid had some kind of trick up his sleeve. But what? How could he trick them now? Nogal was close on his trail and he himself was headed for Jacoby's, where, if the Kid tried going there for horses, he would be waiting.

Could the Apache Kid trick Nogal, he asked himself. And the answer was that, despite Nogal's skill and wisdom on the trail, the Kid was even smarter. Yes, the Kid could trick Nogal.

But they had made their plans and there was nothing to do now but carry them out. He would go to Jacoby's and wait, for at least the rest of today and all of tonight. By dawn, if the Kid still had not appeared, he could assume that somehow, some way, the Kid had outsmarted Nogal, killed him or perhaps put him afoot. He'd put Jacoby on guard and would ride back as fast as he could toward the place he had left Nogal.

He reached Jacoby's in late afternoon, relieved to find not only Jacoby and his wife present, but three drifters who, expecting the Kid to come this way anyhow, eagerly agreed to stay on for the chance of getting a crack at him.

Healy, who knew Jacoby from the days when they both worked for the cavalry, went to the corral with him and made a trade, four fresh horses for his two worn-out ones. Jacoby put the three drifters on guard over the corral, stationing one in the barn loft with a rifle, another in a gulch directly opposite, and the third in a lean-to shed that was attached to the main building but faced the corral, also armed with a high-powered rifle. All three had instructions to shoot first and ask questions afterward. Any Indian or stranger who approached the corral was to be shot on sight. He had three horses saddled and tied within the barn, in case they missed or wounded the

Kid and had to pursue him. Healy put his own four horses in stalls in the barn, saddled and bridled but with the cinches loose. At six o'clock he was as ready as he was ever going to be.

At Jacoby's that night he had the first solid meal since the one he'd had at the San Carlos Agency. He, Jacoby and his wife ate first. Then they took the drifters' guard positions and the three drifters came in and ate.

The drifters were cowhands, looking for jobs. Healy told them, 'I've got a ranch over in western New Mexico. If any one of you kills the Apache Kid, he's got a job with me as long as he wants it.'

They brightened at that and he knew the prospects of a permanent summer and winter job would help keep them awake. He himself found a place in a pile of hay in the barn, lay down and quickly went to sleep.

He awakened a little after midnight. He called out softly to the man on guard in the barn, 'Anything yet?'

'Nope. Not a sign. You figure he'll come in the dark?'

'He'll come when you least expect him to. And that's in the dark.'

It was true that the Kid would do what was least expected of him. But Healy didn't really think he'd come in the dark. The Kid always wanted the advantage and he wouldn't have it, coming into a strange place in the dark. No.

The Kid would probably come at first light, when he could see a little and when he could pick the best of the horses in the corral. He would kill if he was shot at or intercepted, but he probably wouldn't risk killing here for pleasure alone.

Healy went back to sleep, but this time it was a sleep of dozing and catnaps, from which he awakened frequently. He was wide awake when the first gray of dawn appeared in the east. He was stationed in the barn door, his Spencer loaded and in his hands, before he could even see the corral.

He was listening—for any unusual sound made by the horses penned up there. They'd hear the Kid, or smell him, long before he was detected by anyone.

The light strengthened and the sky in the east turned pink. The rising sun stained the few scattered clouds a reddish orange. But the Kid didn't come.

The sun came up at last and Healy knew the Kid wasn't going to come. He got his horses, cinched down the saddles on the first two and tied the others to the tails of the packhorse and the one immediately behind.

He was troubled now by a strong and pervasive uneasiness. Nogal was dead, he thought. He had engaged the Kid and he had lost. So too was Nora, killed in the Kid's blind rage over the enlistment of Nogal.

He warned Jacoby to be on guard. Then he

set out at a lope, his four horses raising a towering cloud of dust.

Yet he did not go straight toward the place he had left Nogal. Instead he circled Jacoby's, a mile out away from it studying the ground minutely for tracks. Not necessarily horse tracks, since the Kid could have approached Jacoby's on foot.

He had expected to find nothing and he found nothing. The Kid had outsmarted him again.

Damn him to hell! He had the instincts of an animal, or the wolverine that lives in the north and can outwit any enemy, even man.

But Healy had caught him once. He could catch him again. If only, pray God, the Kid hadn't killed either Nogal or Nora.

The big trouble was, and Healy recognized it in himself, that he was getting desperate. He knew Nora must be nearly exhausted. Frustration at his inability to catch up with the Kid had added to his sense of recklessness. Things were turning, now. The Kid always had possessed the advantage because he'd had Nora. Now his advantage was increasing hour by hour, day by day.

Healy gripped his hands into fists. He forced himself to calm, forced his feeling of frustration to go away.

After all, damn it, the Kid was just a man. He was subject to all the weaknesses of men, even if to a diminished degree. He could be caught!

CHAPTER THIRTEEN

Nogal followed the Kid's trail south, swiftly but watchfully. Nobody could ever tell what the Kid was going to do. He was capable of letting you think he was circling to lay an ambush farther back along the trail and then lay one here where you least expected it.

The land was nearly flat. There were distant mountains on all sides, but Nogal remembered one particular small cluster of rocks about half a dozen miles back along the trail.

That was where the ambush would be laid. Nogal continued until he found the place where the Kid and Nora had turned west and here he dismounted, having decided that his guess as to the ambush site had been correct. He tied his horses securely to clumps of brush and then, with the sun low in the western sky, again took up the trail of the Apache Kid, this time on foot, running tirelessly.

Nogal was good and knew he was. But he knew the Kid was better at this business of playing cat and mouse across a thousand square miles of desert and mountains. He traveled nearly half a dozen miles before the trail turned north. It was dusk now. The sun was down and all its glow had faded from the clouds.

Nogal ran on. The pile of rocks was plainly visible now and he slowed, approaching as carefully as a stalking animal. Gun ready, held across his chest but capable of being brought into instant play, he reached the rocks. He stopped and pressed himself close against one of them.

Suddenly, he heard the drum of horses' hoofs. And the Kid's taunt in the Apache tongue. 'I hope you have hidden your family well, Nogal. Because if you have not, they are already dead.'

Instantly Nogal broke into a run. Heading toward the sound, he ran harder and faster than he had ever run in his life before. He knew he had been seen and outwitted by the Apache Kid. Worse, he had been recognized. And now he was about to lose his horses. Run as he might, he could never catch the Kid and Nora on their relatively fresh mounts.

But only he knew exactly where his horses were. The Kid would have to grope around in the darkness and find them by sound or smell. And so he continued to run.

The sounds he made running made it impossible for him to hear those of the two horses ridden by Nora and the Kid. Nogal was tough and he was strong. He could run for miles, pacing a loping horse. But the Kid had his horses at a dead run, and no man can keep up with that.

It seemed forever to him. He thought of his

wife and son and knew how precarious was their hiding place. The Kid could find it. If no one would tell him where it was, a few cuts with his razor-sharp knife in the flesh of one of their children and his friends would tell. So he couldn't count on his family being safe. Unless he could reach them before the Apache Kid.

The Kid had a double purpose now, a chance for a doubly sweet revenge. He had Nora, whom he surely intended to kill in the most horrible way possible. In less than twelve hours, he would also have Nogal's wife and boy. Whether he would kill them outright or torture them depended only on the time available.

Nogal reached the place where his horses had been tied. They were not there. But he could hear, diminishing in the distance, the pound of many hoofs.

Indians, especially Apaches, are supposed to be inscrutable, capable of concealing their feelings, however strong they are. But now Nogal was alone, with a thousand square miles of desert surrounding him.

He wept because now he faced the near certainty that his wife and son would be killed.

But he was too tough to grieve for long. The Kid had not killed Nora yet. Perhaps he would not kill Nogal's wife and son, but would kidnap them too, wanting to inflict greater worry and uncertainty.

Less than a minute after the sounds of the horses' hoofs had died away, Nogal was running again, this time straight east, toward Jacoby's Ranch.

He had already run close to a dozen miles. Now he must run at least a dozen more. At daylight he figured Healy would head west toward the place they had separated. Healy would have horses and would be raising dust. Nogal must be sure he saw that dust and that they did not pass without seeing each other.

There would be no further need to trail the Apache Kid because Nogal knew exactly where he was going. But there was a telegraph at the San Carlos Agency. And there were telegraph instruments at every small station along the railroad and in every town. Perhaps they could reach one of them without going too far out of the way and get a telegraph message off to the San Carlos Agency. Nogal had friends among the Apaches there, men with whom he had scouted in the past. They could be counted on to protect his family. If the message got to them in time.

The night seemed endless and so did the distance that he ran. But as last he saw the faint line of gray outlining the horizon ahead of him.

On he ran, while the light strengthened and the eastern sky turned pink. He knew this country well and knew exactly where Jacoby's was. He took bearings occasionally, satisfying himself that he was still maintaining a direct line between the place the Kid had stolen his horses and Jacoby's Ranch.

Nogal did not have a watch and had no need for one. But a couple of hours after first light touched the sky, he saw a rising cloud of dust in the distance and knew that Healy was coming.

The Kid had outwitted both of them. Healy had thought he'd hit Jacoby's for fresh horses and he hadn't. Nogal had thought he could penetrate the Kid's ambush without being discovered and he had also failed.

They were running out of time and they had used up all the mistakes they were going to be allowed.

Healy did not slow his horses as he approached Nogal. Running, Nogal swiftly untied the rear horse from the tail of the one in front and, using only the halter rope to guide him, rode up beside Healy at a dead run, barebacked.

Healy yelled, 'What happened?'

'He tried to lay an ambush for you. He didn't know it was me on his trail and I passed the place he'd picked for the ambush before he could circle and get back to it. I went back afoot but I am getting to be a clumsy old man. He saw me and recognized me and then he rode out and stole my horses before I could get back to them.'

'What do you figure he's up to now?'

'He is going to San Carlos. He will find my wife and son and kill them both. Unless we can get there first, or unless we can reach a telegraph and send a message to San Carlos telling my friends that I have scouted with to find my family and protect them from him.'

'How long will it take the Kid to find your family?'

Nogal shrugged expressively. 'His sharp knife at the throat of an Apache baby will very quickly get him the information he wants.'

'Then we've got to find a telegraph.'

There was a railroad station at Foley. That was where Lieutenant MacBrayer was with his small detachment of cavalry.

Healy said, 'Foley's closest. And there's another telegraph operator there now.'

He turned his horse slightly to head straight for the Foley railroad station. Nogal, his face as inscrutable as ever despite the worry that must be nearly driving him insane, kept pace.

* * *

Healy knew he was taking a chance the instant the decision was made to forget the Kid's trail and ride to the Foley railroad depot. It was Nogal's guess that the Kid would head straight for San Carlos, but Healy was not so sure. There was one thing you could depend upon in the Apache Kid and that was that he would do what you least expected him to do. If he had threatened Nogal and told him he was heading for San Carlos to kill his family, that didn't necessarily mean that was what he was going to do.

But, having put Nogal afoot and gained a good start on them, it was likely that he *would* go to San Carlos. And anyway, after they had sent their telegraph message to San Carlos, they could ride up the valley and perhaps pick the Kid's trail up where he crossed the road or the railroad tracks.

Healy maintained a steady lope in a northeasterly direction. San Carlos was over a hundred miles from where Nogal had been set afoot. The Kid could reach it before dark today.

Foley was probably thirty miles from Jacoby's Ranch, a little less from where they were right now. Now and then Healy glanced back at Nogal. He wished he could reassure the scout but he could not. The Kid might have stopped and cut the telegraph lines as he passed beneath them on his way north. If he did, it would mean no word of his coming could precede his arrival at San Carlos. Nogal's wife and son would die.

But, thought Healy, maybe San Carlos was where the Kid meant for it to end.

He shook his head immediately. The Kid had no intention of letting this end in a place as well populated as San Carlos was. The Kid wanted it to end out in the trackless desert, fifty miles from the nearest settlement. Healy had to admit, reluctantly to himself, that the chances of Nogal's wife and son were not very good. And it was his fault. He had asked Nogal to go with him. He had placed Nogal's wife and son in jeopardy.

Then he shook his head almost imperceptibly. No. Nogal himself had placed them in jeopardy when he joined the band of scouts that Healy led on the Apache Kid's trail two years ago. Furthermore, when the Kid was through with Nogal and with Healy, it was likely that he would seek revenge against each of the other scouts that had gone along that time.

He had to be killed, and soon. If they could only reach the telegraph before the Kid cut the wires. Healy raked his horse savagely with his spurs but the animal was running at full speed and could go no faster than he already was.

It seemed forever before they saw the railroad tracks ahead. And the water tank, dwarfed by distance, and the tiny station and telegrapher's office. They were half a mile away before men came out on the station platform and stared at them. MacBrayer's men, Healy thought.

He didn't know what gods Nogal prayed to, if he, indeed, prayed to any. But he himself was praying soundlessly that they would be in time, that the Kid would either have neglected to cut the wires or wouldn't have reached them yet, even though that seemed unlikely as hell.

They rode to the station at full speed and dust rolled past them and obscured MacBrayer and the troopers standing on the platform with him. Healy yelled, 'The telegraph! Are the wires cut?'

MacBrayer shook his head. Healy hit the ground running and leaped onto the platform. He rushed inside.

To the telegrapher he said, 'Don't write this down. Put it on the wire as I give it to you. "Agent, San Carlos Indian Reservation. Urgent."' The instrument began to click busily. Healy opened his mouth to speak again and suddenly there was silence in the room. The telegrapher clicked his key rapidly and then looked back at Healy with puzzlement in his eyes. 'I get no acknowledgment. I think the line's been cut.'

'Keep trying.'

The telegrapher clicked his key rapidly, then waited. Nothing happened. The silence in the room seemed deafening. Healy grabbed a pad of yellow telegraph blanks and swiftly wrote his message on it. He shoved it at the telegrapher. 'Keep trying. The line's been cut but I'm going down the line and try to splice it together again. Have you got a piece of wire six or eight feet long?'

The man got up, dug around in a corner and handed Healy a piece of wire. Healy said, 'Pincers?'

The telegrapher gave him a pair.

Healy went outside. He found it hard to meet Nogal's eyes. He said, 'He's cut the wire. But maybe if we get there quickly we can splice it together again. The message might still reach San Carlos before he does.'

Nogal's face showed no emotion, but his eyes turned dull. Healy went back into the station. To the telegrapher he said. 'Lives depend on that message. You send it the minute your instrument's working again.'

'Yes sir.'

Healy laid a twenty-dollar gold piece on the counter. He went out again. MacBrayer asked, 'Anything I can do?'

Healy shook his head. 'He's headed for San Carlos to kill Nogal's family. He's cut the telegraph wire but we're going to try and splice it. You can see to it that that message I left goes out as soon as it gets fixed.'

MacBrayer nodded. But Healy was already on his horse. He spurred away up the railroad tracks, with his string of horses keeping pace and with Nogal no more than a dozen yards behind.

CHAPTER FOURTEEN

Healy rode along beneath the telegraph wires recklessly, glancing at each span to make sure it was still intact. He didn't know how the Kid could have cut the wire. He must have found a sharp edge of rock and sawed it through. He made no attempt to save the horses' strength.

All he could think of was Nogal's wife and son.

Suddenly, ahead, Healy saw a missing span of wire between two poles. He pulled up to a plunging halt, to be overrun by the horses he was leading. Nogal was already off his horse.

Healy asked, 'Can you climb the pole?'

Nogal nodded wordlessly.

Healy went to the end of the length of wire lying on the ground. He picked it up and with his pocketknife, stripped off the insulation. He bent it around his lariat, then similarly stripped the piece they had brought along for splicing. He handed the other end of the rope with the two wires bent around it to Nogal and the squat Apache started scrambling up the pole. He did it skilfully, with the rope looped around his waist. When he reached the top, he first skinned the insulation off the dangling wire, then proceeded to splice the piece to it and then to splice the piece to the long length that had been lying on the ground. He shook it back and forth a couple of times to make sure wind wouldn't break it loose again, then came down the pole like a monkey.

There was nothing more they could do here. The line was fixed and if the telegrapher did what he'd been told, and Healy felt sure MacBrayer would see to it he did, the message about the Kid's coming should be going out over the wires soon if it was not already doing so. The Indian Agent would be warned and he in turn would warn the Apaches who had served as scouts two years ago. Nogal's family should be safe.

Nogal now took the lead and Healy permitted it, knowing Nogal was much more familiar than he was with the terrain between here and San Carlos and also that he could probably save time, a minute, five, fifteen. But every hour, he yelled at Nogal and they stopped long enough to change their saddles from the horses they were riding to the barebacked ones. At one point, Healy turned the packhorse loose, but the animal followed them, nearly keeping pace, although nothing forced him to except perhaps a reluctance to be left alone.

Now the hours dragged, and became frustrating because both of them knew they had done and were doing all they could. The telegraph message had been sent, or at least they had done their part to make sure it was. Now all they could do was ride, forcing their horses to their maximum speed without taking the risk of killing them.

They had long since given up trying to follow the Kid's trail. This bothered Healy because he knew how unpredictable the Kid was. He was capable of making them think he was heading for San Carlos while he rode in the opposite direction. Heading for San Carlos might ensure the safety of Nogal's family but if the Kid went some other way, Nora was in greater danger than before.

It was a couple of hours after dark before the

pair reached San Carlos. Nogal headed immediately for the place he'd left his wife and son. Healy took a moment to ride by the telegraph office. No lamp burned inside. It was dark and so were the Agent's quarters. He cursed savagely to himself, then swung his horse and headed after Nogal. He had fallen behind and could no longer see the Apache scout, but he could hear him and he followed him by sound.

He had no way of knowing how long the telegraph instrument here had been unmanned. The message so vital to Nogal and his family might have clicked away in an empty office, over and over again, until the sender at Foley finally gave up.

There was some kind of commotion down among the wickiups of the Apaches. Nogal ignored it, heading into the hills north of the Agency. But curiosity drew Healy to the gathering and to the fires that, at this hour, had usually been killed.

There was a light spring wagon among the fires, hitched to a single team. Some of the Apaches were grieving, singing the strange, minor-key death chant that Healy had heard before. Others sat beside the fires, staring inscrutably into them.

Healy rode to the wagon. No attempt had been made to cover the body, as white men would have done. The dead Indian was a man, one of the Apaches who had scouted with him two years ago, one named Chavez. Healy had seen the Kid's work before, but the horror of this made him turn his head away.

He knew instantly why Chavez was dead. Chavez had known the location of Nogal's family. The Kid had managed to take him and tie him and had then proceeded to get the information he wanted out of him.

Healy had no illusions that Chavez had not told. No man could stand the things the Kid had done to him and keep silent.

There was a piece of canvas in the back of the wagon. Healy covered Chavez with it. He knew he ought to go after Nogal, but he also knew that Nogal was, by now, too far ahead of him. He'd never catch up and besides, the Apache Kid was long gone. Nogal would want to be alone with the bodies of his wife and son.

They'd have to wait for morning anyway. Harvey Cobb, the Agent, would probably want to give Chavez and Nogal's wife and son a Christian burial. But Healy wouldn't wait for that. Nor would Nogal. As much as Healy, he would want to be on the trail as soon as it was light enough to find it and follow it. Nogal had adopted many of the white man's ways, but a Christian burial would mean nothing to him. He would prefer to be on the trail of the man who had killed the two and who had tortured Chavez until he revealed their whereabouts.

Healy waited anxiously for nearly an hour before Nogal came riding into the firelight. The fires had begun to die, and the chanting had ceased. Healy's eyes went instantly to the horse that Nogal was trailing, nearly holding his breath for fear he would see Nora's body there.

But there was only one body tied on the horse's back. Nogal carried the slight, small body of his son in his arms.

Healy was ashamed of the long, deep sigh of relief that escaped his lips. Then he was beside Nogal, taking the boy's body from him, trying not to look at the torture the Kid had inflicted before his final knife thrust killed the boy. But in spite of himself he saw enough to make his brain grow hot with fury and hatred, and he saw more when he helped Nogal untie and lift the body of his wife from the horse's back.

Apache women came and took the bodies into one of the wickiups. Some other women, after obtaining permission from Nogal, took Chavez in too. Healy wouldn't have blamed Nogal if he'd held Chavez's betrayal against him. But he apparently did not.

Nogal paced nervously back and forth among the fires. Healy said, 'We will be leaving at first light. You should eat. And you should rest. I will get fresh horses at the stable.'

Finally Nogal nodded. He lay down beside one of the fires and closed his eyes. Healy didn't know whether he was asleep or not.

He mounted his horse and led his extra horses and Nogal's toward the stable at the Agency.

Like the Agent's quarters and the telegraph office, it was dark. He went inside, struck a match and lighted a lantern hanging by the door. Slim came stumbling out of the tack room rubbing his eyes. Healy asked, 'How long has that damn telegraph office been closed?'

'All day. The telegrapher went to Tucson. He'll be gone a couple more days.'

Healy cursed. Slim glanced at him questioningly, but Healy didn't explain. There wasn't any use. The damage was done and three people were dead because the telegrapher had selected today to go to Tucson. Healy said, 'I want six horses. It's going to have to be on credit because damn near all my money is gone. And the people at the next place I stop for horses might not know I was good for them.'

'Help yourself.'

'Huh uh. You know your horses. You get me the six best ones. I'll hold the lantern for you.'

He followed Slim out, carrying the lantern. Slim asked, 'What happened? Did the Kid come here?'

'Yeah. Killed Chavez and Nogal's family.'

Slim shook his head slowly, but did not reply. He was busy. He had the horses in the corral thundering a circle inside of it. Every now and then his rope snaked out and he pulled a horse out of the herd. He tied each to the corral gate by halter and halter rope, all of which he took from nails hanging from the gate.

In ten minutes, six horses were tied to the gate. Healy led them out, one by one. He saddled two, one for Nogal, one for himself. The packhorse had caught up, so he took off the pack and put it on the back of one of the fresh horses. He dug out the sack, filled it with oats in the stable and put it back. Slim asked, 'You got enough to eat?'

'Nogal will bring some jerky.'

'You're losin' weight.'

'Maybe. But Nora is too.'

'She's still . . .' It was dark and Healy couldn't see Slim's face, but by the way Slim stammered afterward, he knew how embarrassed he was.

He said, 'She's still alive. That goddam Kid has got something special planned for Nora and me.'

There was now nothing much to be done until first light. Healy tied an extra horse to the packhorse's tail, and one to the tail of the horse Nogal would lead. He waited, then, with Slim, keeping his eye on the horizon in the east. He hoped Nogal would have gotten some sleep, or at least some rest. But how do you sleep and how do you rest after seeing the things that have been done to your wife and son?

The Kid was building up a reservoir of hatred that would drown him eventually. Only they had to catch him first.

Healy didn't worry about awakening Nogal. He knew the Apache awakened every morning at first light. By the time it was light enough to trail, Nogal would be here, with his weapons and with a sack of jerky given him by the reservation Indians. He would be ready to go.

Gray finally lightened the eastern sky. Nogal arrived, carrying his short-barreled trapdoor rifle and a sack of jerky. Healy mounted his horse, very anxious now to go. He had been able to think of only Nora for the past several hours. And to wonder what was in the Apache Kid's mind.

They had no trail, and around the San Carlos Agency were hundreds of separate trails, coming and going. But since south was probably the direction the Kid would choose, they rode south until they were a mile from the Agency. Then Healy said, 'You go right and I'll go left. Fire your gun if you pick it up.'

He dismounted and, leading his horses, bending low, studied the ground as he walked. Even this far from the Agency, there were many trails, but most of them were old.

He had traveled more than a mile before he found it, a trail of two horses, hard-ridden, with the edges of their hoofprints still sharp and even, in some places, damp. Healy immediately raised the Spencer, pointed it in Nogal's general direction and fired it.

Then he waited, studying the hoofprints of the Kid's horses as someone else might study the fine print in a book. From the depth of the hoofprints of the second horse, he judged that

Nora was still with the Kid.

He wished desperately that he could see her, could see what condition she was in. And he felt a surge of admiration run through him for her strength and stamina. Any other woman would have been dead by now. But Nora was still riding, maybe strengthened by her hatred of the butcher she was riding with.

But what did it matter, the source of her strength? What she had to do was remain alive until Healy and Nogal could catch the Kid.

Healy could have become discouraged, but he wouldn't let himself. They would catch the Kid. They would rescue Nora. And the Kid would get what was coming to him.

CHAPTER FIFTEEN

The Apache Kid had changed horses, so it was impossible for Healy to recognize the hoofprints and therefore to be sure these tracks had been made by the Kid. He waited until Nogal arrived and then pointed to the tracks. 'He changed horses. I think it's him but I can't be sure. What do you think?'

Nogal dismounted and squatted to study the tracks. He moved along, occasionally touching a track with his forefinger. When he rose he said, 'No can be sure, but I think it him. You want to follow or go back where he stole horses and make sure?'

Healy frowned, trying to decide. It was very unlikely that any Apache had left the reservation at a run last night, trailing another horse. Possible but unlikely. And it would take two hours at the very least to return to the wickiups and find out from whom the Kid had stolen his horses. It might take longer, because whoever the horses had been stolen from might be dead.

Healy said, 'I think it's him. There's somebody on the second horse and whoever's on the first is leading it. To me, that adds up to the Kid.'

Nogal nodded agreement. He said, 'If you decide to go back, I would have gone on.'

Healy and Nogal mounted and set out at a gallop, following the tracks of the two strange horses south. The farther they went, the more certain they became that they were right. The pace the two horses were maintaining was certainly an indication that the Kid was riding one of them.

Healy found it almost unbelievable that Nogal's expression was no different than it had been yesterday. It was still grim, intent. The grief he was most certainly feeling was hidden behind that grimness.

And yet there was a vague something in his eyes that had not been there yesterday, something that made Healy glad he was not the object of Nogal's quest. That look in Nogal's eyes was a promise of death that would not and could not be broken until Nogal himself was dead.

My God, he thought, how could Nora continue to stand up under the hardships she was subjected to? His throat tightened and his eyes burned and the love and admiration he had for her increased with every mile. If it was humanly possible, she would survive. She had been tied and beaten and no doubt raped but she had made up her mind that she would survive. And survive she would unless the Kid took a notion to torture and kill her outright, which was unlikely since the Kid didn't even know how far behind he and Nogal were. Besides, he had slaked his bloodthirst on Nogel's wife and son last night.

He remembered their bodies and he wondered what kind of monster could mutilate, torture and kill a woman and small boy the way he had.

And he knew that no matter how many horses they wore out and killed, no matter how they rode or how hard they pushed themselves, the Kid's rampage of murder was not over with. He would kill again, and again, before he could be stopped.

*   *   *

Nora had no idea when the Kid reached the outskirts of San Carlos what he wanted there.

But she submitted to being tied, trying to hold both her wrists and ankles so that there would be some slack in the thongs he was tying her with.

She managed a little slack, but not much. There was no chance she could free herself no matter how long the Kid stayed away. He mounted his own horse and, leading hers, rode toward the Apache village a few miles from the Agency.

Lying there, having made herself as comfortable as possible and arranged both arms and legs so that circulation stoppage was minimal, she let herself wonder what the Kid was doing here. He had cut the telegraph line south of here, which, to her, meant he wanted to keep a warning from being sent by telegraph to the Agency. That meant he intended to kill somebody. But who?

Not the Agent, certainly. The Agent had had nothing to do with the Kid's incarceration in Florida. And it was unlikely that he bore enough animosity toward any other white at the Agency to go out of his way to murder him.

It followed, therefore, that his target had to be another Apache. One or more of the Apache scouts who had helped Frank run him to earth two years ago.

One name instantly came to her. Nogal. He had been the one closest to Frank, the best tracker of them all. If the Kid blamed anybody besides Frank for being caught and sent to

Florida, it would be Nogal. Besides, back at the ambush site south of here, she had heard the Kid call out Nogal's name. He had been speaking in Apache, which she did not understand, but that one word had been unmistakable.

And since Nogal had been at the ambush site, where the Kid had stolen his horses, it followed that he could not possibly be at the Agency now. So the Kid must be after Nogal's family. By killing them he could hurt the scout ten times more than he could by torturing and killing Nogal himself. And the Kid wanted to hurt . . . Frank Healy. Nogal. The other scouts who had helped catch him two years ago. When he wasn't busy killing people he had never even seen before.

She stared into the darkness, waiting, knowing what the Kid was doing and helpless to do anything about it. An hour passed and more. The only way she had of judging time was by the moon and stars, something Frank had taught her when they were courting and walking alone at night.

Finally the Kid returned. She knew he had before she heard him. One minute she was alone, the next she knew he had returned. Perhaps it was a smell, perhaps a sound, felt as much as heard, or even a slight vibration in the ground.

He untied her, and she could smell the fresh blood on him. The compulsion to scream and claw and fight him until he killed her too was almost irresistible. But she resisted it, forcing herself to think of all the terrible miles that lay behind, of all the dead the Kid must account for, and of Frank, who was coming, just as certainly as was the Judgment Day. She would only cheat Frank if she let him arrive to find her dead. And she would cheat the child she knew she carried now.

The Kid had fresh horses he had undoubtedly stolen at the Agency. She mounted obediently.

Her thighs and seat were calloused now and used to the twelve or fourteen hours a day that she must endure. But she had lost weight, perhaps ten or fifteen pounds. Part of this was water loss, but at least two thirds of it was actual weight loss. She looked down at her breasts, regretting their diminished size and thinking of Frank as she did. If and when she was rescued, she would put her mind to getting the lost weight back on, for her unborn baby's sake, but also for her own and Frank's. No man liked making love to a stick.

How would he feel about her being raped by the Apache Kid, she wondered. She hoped desperately that he would understand that it had been just another part of surviving. But a woman never knew how a man was going to react.

And would he think their child had been sired by the Kid during the rape? It was possible. But it would not be possible after the child was born. He would be too fair to have any Indian blood. But by then perhaps the damage would be done.

She rode south behind the Kid, remembering the way he had been while he untied the thongs that bound her hands and feet. All the hard tension seemed to have gone out of him. His hands, untying the thongs, had not been unnecessarily cruel. She thought furiously that torture and murder had the same effect on the Kid that lovemaking had on a normal man.

In his relaxed state, she realized that she was relatively safe from him. Now all he wanted to do was put miles between himself and the scene of his latest atrocity.

She felt her anger growing as she thought of Nogal's wife and son, now dead. The killing lust came periodically to the Kid the way need for a woman came periodically to normal men. And he never failed to find someone upon whom he could satisfy it.

They traveled at either a lope or a run for the better part of the night, always south. Nora knew that Frank and Nogal couldn't trail at night. She also knew how far behind the Kid they must have been. They would probably not pick up the trail until daylight made it possible.

As light began to streak the sky, the Kid halted beside a narrow stream. He let the horses suck up water noisily until he thought they'd had enough and then pulled them away from the stream by force. He knew exactly how far he was ahead of Frank and Nogal, Nora thought. He probably wasn't sure how soon he could replace the horses so he was going to let them rest awhile.

She dismounted. For some reason, perhaps that he didn't intend to sleep, the Kid did not tie her hands and feet. He waited awhile, then let the horses drink again. This time they stopped of their own accord.

He tied them to a couple of clumps of stout brush, then without speaking to her, lay down on the ground nearby. Nora wasted no time. She lay down too, closed her eyes and tried to sleep.

But the vision of Nogal's wife and child kept parading before her thoughts and she couldn't sleep. Finally she opened her eyes and stared at the Kid. His eyes were closed, his body relaxed. As she watched, he shifted position very slightly and snored.

She knew that a snore does not mean deep sleep. She also knew how tired the Kid must be. And she wasn't tied. Maybe now her chance had come to do *something*, something that would help her husband to catch up.

Slowly, with extreme care to make no noise, she got to her knees and afterward to her feet. All this time her eyes were fixed upon the Kid. He didn't move.

Carefully, testing and studying each place

where she would put down her foot, she moved toward the horses. She was terrified and trembling violently because she knew what would happen to her if the Kid awoke. But this was the first chance she'd had to do something and she wasn't going to let it pass.

She reached the horses. Still the Kid slept. With extreme care, she unbuckled the bridle from the first one, then moved to the second and unbuckled his bridle too. The horses now were loose, saddled but free to go.

Carefully she placed a rein around the neck of each, and as carefully led them, knowing they would not step as carefully as she, away from the temporary camp.

The Kid still had not moved. One of the horses stepped on a branch and it cracked with a sound that seemed thunderous. The Kid stirred and Nora knew he was on the verge of waking up.

It was now or never. She released both horses and with the bridle she still held in her hand, lashed them as hard as she could across their rumps, at the same time screaming as shrilly and as loudly as she could. What she hoped was that the horses, so suddenly freed, would head for the Agency from which they had been stolen earlier.

Both horses took off at a lope, startled and frightened by her scream. But now the Kid was up. He passed her and as he did, swung a powerful arm. His closed hand struck her in the mouth and knocked her sprawling to the ground. Then both horses and the Apache Kid were gone.

Nora knew she would be foolish to wait here for the Kid to return. If he recovered the horses, she could expect a severe beating if nothing worse. If he did not recover the horses, she could expect death, probably a slow death because he would be so furious at what she had done.

She began to run, trying her best to hide her trail by stepping on rocks and clumps of brush but knowing all the time that attempts to hide a trail from the Apache Kid were a waste of time.

But there *was* a chance . . . that he would pursue the horses on foot long enough for her to put a substantial distance between himself and their temporary camp. She was terrified that he would kill her for what she had done. But she was willing to accept a beating, so long as he did not strike her in the abdomen and cause a miscarriage of her child.

For a time there was silence, broken only by the unavoidable noises she made in fleeing the spot. She could hear neither the Apache Kid nor the horses he was pursuing. But she could imagine his towering rage, and she wished frantically she had not done what she had done. She should have relied on Frank to catch up and deal with the Apache Kid himself. He was better equipped and better qualified.

She prayed, 'O God, let the horses keep on running toward home. Let him fail to catch them, and let me get away.' Frank and Nogal, if they were still together, would pick up her trail almost as quickly as would the Kid. They would find her and then she would be safe.

And yet, she could not bring herself to believe this. Her faith in her prayers was weak. The Kid would catch the horses because it was not the nature of horses to run for very long unless something was forcing them. He would return and pick up her trail and he would be in a towering rage when he did. If she did not get killed it would be a miracle.

Terror made her careless and she stopped trying to hide her trail. It wouldn't do any good anyway. The Kid could read any trail that she might try to hide as easily as a white man read a book.

At last, exhausted, she sank to the ground, overheated and breathing raggedly. She waited, having concealed herself as best she could. She continued to pray, but without any real faith.

She heard the hoofbeats of the horses. Shortly thereafter she saw them, the Kid riding one and leading the other.

Her hiding of herself was as ineffective as her hiding of her trail had been. He saw her as easily as if she had been in the open.

He said nothing, but his eyes were narrowed and murderous. Nora thought, 'Now I am going to die.' And, despite the ineffectiveness of her earlier prayers, she prayed that her death would be quick, and not drawn out with torture as were the deaths of so many of the Apache Kid's victims.

He was off his horse. She stood and faced him, her mouth set firmly, her eyes trying desperately to be unafraid.

Reaching her, he swung a fist that took her squarely in the mouth. Lips smashed and blood spurted from them. She staggered back and sat down helplessly. Before he could reach her, she made an attempt to get to her feet, protecting her abdomen where the baby was with her folded arms. His fist smashed her again, this time on the side of the head. Again she went to the ground, assuming a fetal position in the hope of protecting her unborn child. She felt his kicks, on her back, her legs, her shoulders and her head. Her consciousness slipped away but she didn't change her position, willing to take whatever punishment he put her through as long as she could protect her belly where the developing child was. At least, it appeared he didn't intend killing her or he'd have already done so.

When he finally stopped, she was a mass of bruises. She hurt from head to toe. He said furiously, 'White bitch, get on your horse. I should kill you but I am not ready yet.' He spoke in English, something he rarely did.

Nora got painfully to her feet. Wincing with

every step, she made her way to her horse and with difficulty mounted him.

Her hurts would heal. The main thing was that she had not been killed. And that none of his kicks or blows had landed on her lower abdomen where the developing baby was.

What she had done had been foolish and had accomplished nothing. But she'd felt she had to try, no matter what the consequences might be.

She would make no more foolish attempts to escape because the Kid's patience was wearing thin. Only his desire to torture and kill her before Frank's eyes had kept him from killing her a few minutes ago.

She had better forget escape. She had better simply endure. And rely on Frank to catch up with the Apache Kid before it was too late.

CHAPTER SIXTEEN

They traveled south, alternating between a rumplashed run and the Kid's customary pace, a lope. To Nora it was beginning to look as if, at last, fear might have touched the Kid. He had murdered Nogal's family and well knew that Nogal could be as fiercely savage as he could himself. He knew Frank would be with Nogal. And that others of the scouts who had caught up with him before might be along.

Nora had accustomed herself to riding. She had lost every bit of excess weight, of which she'd had very little to spare anyway. She had been badly beaten and kicked, until every part of her body hurt, and she was beginning to tire. The miles and the days seemed to stretch endlessly ahead with only one thing certain, that the Kid could cover a hundred of those miles a day and his pursuers would have to do better if they expected to catch up with him.

For some reason she did not understand, the Kid seemed more savage than he had before. His face, certainly never mobile, was even more set in its angry mold. And his eyes . . . They frightened her, so fierce and murderous were they.

She puzzled over the change. The only thing different now was that he had murdered, and probably tortured, Nogal's wife and son. Was it possible that the Apache Kid had a conscience, that its pangs were the reason for his increased angry savagery?

Possible. Anything was possible. But she didn't believe it. All the Kid would understand was fear.

They traveled hard all day, until near dark the horses began stumbling. But the Kid seemed to know exactly where he was going, and as the last light began fading from the sky, they brought into sight a small adobe building with a sod roof. There were a windmill and corral nearby, and in the corral were half a dozen horses.

Now someone else would die, she thought, and hoped desperately that nobody was here. The Kid did something surprising. He pulled her horse forward and before she realized what he was doing, whipped the red piece of cloth from around his forehead, forced it into her mouth and tied it painfully tight behind. Then he rode forward, taking her with him. He was going to make her watch the killings, she thought, and shuddered at the prospect, feeling the blood drain from her face. It was bad enough to know that people were being slaughtered and sometimes tortured. But it would be infinitely worse to be forced to watch.

He approached the place from the rear, where there were no windows. She could see, as darkness deepened, the faint glow from a light or two falling on the ground in front. It was hot and the door was probably open. And there were probably a couple of windows on that side, which faced the north.

They had reached the building before one of the horses in the corral smelled their two horses and nickered. The Kid's horse tried to reply, but the Kid clamped a cruel hand over his nostrils and cut it off. Nora's horse gave an answering nicker, however, which she made no attempt to stifle.

The Kid was off his horse instantly. Crouching, silent, he rounded the adobe shack on the side away from the corral. Always thinking, he knew that when one of the occupants stepped outside, he would be facing the corral from which the sounds had come.

There was a scuffle, but Nora stayed where she was. She could do nothing to help the hapless inhabitants of this small house. She could not scream or speak. And if she tried to intervene physically the Kid would kill her instantly.

She heard a thud, like something striking a human head, then a woman's scream from inside the house. Almost immediately a child began to cry hysterically.

Nora could stand no more of it. She was very near hysteria herself and she suddenly didn't care anymore whether the Kid killed her or not. He was *not* going to force her to watch while he slaughtered a man, his wife and tiny child, even if she died for resisting him.

Her hands were not tied. Her horse wore no bridle, only a halter, and the halter rope was trailing on the ground. She leaned forward as far as she could and got hold of the halter rope. Then, kicking her horse with her heels and guiding him with the halter rope, she rode away from the tiny shack into the darkness. She tried to kick the horse into a lope, but the best she could get out of him was a sluggish walk. The horse was exhausted, ruined and probably near death. Her chance of getting away from the Kid on him was non-existent.

So she stopped, three hundred yards out into

the darkness, far enough, and upwind, so that she could not hear the sounds from the house. To ensure that she did not, she raised her hands and put them over her ears.

She looked up at the star-studded, beautiful night sky. She heard a coyote yelping on a nearby knoll. Desperately she asked her God how he could let a monster like the Apache Kid survive.

She waited, on the dark side of the house, unable to see what was happening in front.

Nora had never really hated anyone or anything in her life. Sometimes, as a girl, she had thought she hated the boys at the Army post who tormented her.

But that had never really been hate at all. Not like this. Not like the flush that came over her entire body, that seemed like a fire burning in her brain, that made her want to see the Kid tied and staked out before her and her with a sharp knife in her hand.

If that ever came to pass, which was unlikely, God would give her the strength to do what she had to do. Kill. Rid the earth of this monster, who killed for pleasure, who killed for convenience, who even killed for no reason at all. A butcher of human flesh. And he would go on and on and on until Nogal and Frank caught up with him. Or, if he succeeding in killing both Nogal and Frank, until a corps of Apache scouts, mobilized by the Army, caught up with him again.

Not again would his life be spared. There would be no confinement for him this time, in Florida or anyplace else.

But he hadn't been caught yet. And the trail of death he was leaving across Arizona Territory still had no end in sight.

She caught a glimpse of him beyond the house at the corral and knew it was all over. She hadn't been forced to watch, but she knew the man, woman and child who had lived in this small adobe house were dead.

Now there was no longer a valid reason for risking her own life and that of her unborn child. She rode toward the house and took up a position behind it, where the Kid had left her.

He came from the corral, leading two fresh horses. Unceremoniously he grabbed her leg and pulled her from her horse, dumping her cruelly on the ground. Swiftly he changed her saddle and bridle from the worn-out horse to the fresh one he had brought from the corral. He whacked her across the shoulders hard enough to stagger her in lieu of a command to mount. She mounted and waited. The Kid cut the worn-out horses's throat and the animal collapsed, gurgling, to the ground.

Nora felt sick. But she said nothing, did nothing. She had courage and if the time ever came when an action of hers might effect the outcome of this chase, she would take it unhesitatingly, regardless of the danger to herself. But she wasn't a fool and she wasn't going to throw away her life in an action nothing more than symbolic and of no practical purpose.

The Kid had already changed his own saddle to a fresh horse, had already slit the throat of the horse he had worn out. He went into the house, so contemptuous of her courage that he did not even bother to tie his horse. He came out with a gunnysack filled with provisions and with a canteen full of water. He mounted, kicked the horse, which was fresh and eager and frightened of his Apache smell, into a lope. Dragged along behind, Nora's horse kept pace.

Not far from the adobe shack, the Kid managed to whip the horses into a dead run. He kept them at this pace for about twenty miles before he halted them and made camp for the night. The horses were heaving, and their hides were covered with foam and sweat.

He made no move to exercise them, or to rub them down, allowing them to cool naturally. This action, or lack of it on his part, led her to believe he was close to another ranch from which he could steal more horses.

He took his red headband out of her mouth and tied her with the leather thongs. She tried to sleep. The Kid lay down twenty feet or so from her while the horses grazed listlessly fifty yards away. One was staked out, which ensured that both would stay in the vicinity.

She could not sleep, thinking of the man, his wife and child who had been murdered, not for these two horses, either. The Kid could have obtained the horses without killing the whole family of the man who owned them.

He had killed them out of pure savagery. Maybe, she thought, he got some kind of perverted pleasure out of murdering.

Oddly enough, the Kid did not sleep as soundly tonight as he usually did. Nora wondered why. The killings hadn't bothered him, of that she was very sure.

Could it be that he was still afraid? Could his murder of Nogal's family have destroyed his arrogance and confidence in himself?

That had to be it, she decided before she finally went into an aching sleep. The Kid knew for certain that Nogal would never leave the trail. Sooner or later he would have to face Nogal, and perhaps others of the Apache scouts who were Nogal's friends. In addition to facing Frank Healy, whose wife he held.

Maybe, at last, the Kid was himself learning the meaning of fear. Fear of death. Fear of torture. Fear of humiliation and failure.

An Apache shows no emotion of any kind. But that does not mean they feel no emotion of any kind. She felt a touch of triumph. She was afraid and so was Frank. But it was comforting to know that the Apache Kid was also afraid. However savage and vicious and murderous he might be, he was still afraid. The realization lifted her spirits, made the ache in her body less and gave her a hope she had not heretofore experienced.

There *was* hope. At least two men and perhaps many more were on her trail, trying to rescue her. Sooner or later the Apache Kid would make a mistake. He would be caught, with exhausted horses, far from a fresh supply. Or he himself would tire, however unlikely that seemed right now.

There could be no rest for him. He must keep going, at close to a hundred miles a day. Because he knew that was the pace his pursuers would maintain.

* * *

The trail, aimless at best, eventually brought the Kid and Nora back to the tiny railroad station at Foley, where MacBrayer waited with his small contingent of troops.

He had sent out daily patrols, hoping one of them would cross the trail of the Apache Kid. None of them had. They came in every night with negative reports.

Lieutenant MacBrayer cursed. Not in front of his men, but in private and under his breath. He felt like someone trying to swat a bothersome fly who would never land on anything long enough for the swatter to smash him.

And, as is inevitably the case with inaction and failure, he eventually grew careless. He was convinced the Apache Kid would not return to this isolated place. Why should he? The horses available here were tall cavalry remounts that would die under the Kid's treatment in less than fifty miles.

Careless, he let his men sleep at night instead of putting them out on sentry duty around the perimeter of the camp. They had ridden hard all day. Why should he tire them further by making them stand guard at night?

The attack came in the middle of the night, unexpectedly and without apparent purpose. Among the sleeping troopers crept the Apache Kid, stifling outcries with a calloused hand clamped over their mouths as he swiftly and efficiently slit the troopers' throats. He killed five before one, scheduled to be next, awoke and gave the alarm.

Then, before they could organize a pursuit, before indeed they even understood what was happening, the Apache Kid was gone, fading into the darkness like a wraith, who cannot be caught, who will not be caught.

MacBrayer cursed long and bitterly, not caring who heard his profanity. But it was too late. Too late to save the five dead troopers whose blood had soaked the ground.

The Kid left the railroad station at Foley with no more feeling apparent in his demeanor than had been there as he approached the place. Nora, who had been left two or three hundred yards from the station, gagged and with her horse tied securely to a clump of brush, heard nothing but the outcry that arose after the troopers discovered the Kid had been in their bivouac and discovered what he had done.

The Kid returned, yanked loose the halter rope of her horse, removed the gag from her mouth and retied it around his head. He had two of the troopers' horses, great, long-legged, thick-barreled thoroughbreds to which he transferred their saddles, halter and bridle. This time he didn't bother to cut the worn-out horses' throats. He rode away, forcing the cavalry remounts into a running gait that ate up the miles at a startling rate.

Normally, she thought, he would have had nothing to do with cavalry remounts. She puzzled over the fact that he was willing to steal them now.

She thought she understood when he rode directly south. At last the Kid was worn out by the chase. He was heading now into Mexico, to Victorio's old strong-hold in the inaccessible Sierra Madre.

He would use and kill these cavalry horses, aware as anyone that they could outrun anything for a short distance of, say, forty or fifty miles. But forty or fifty miles would put him in Mexico at the foot of the Sierra Madre.

There, he could steal burros from Mexican villagers. And the foot-sure, rugged little animals would take them up the impossible mountain trails.

There was no way for her to know what the Kid intended to do with her now. She would have to wait, and pray.

CHAPTER SEVENTEEN

Lieutenant MacBrayer awakened to the yells of his men, to the sound of useless gunshots fired aimlessly into the dark. It took him only a minute to discover what had happened and then his hoarse voice roared for the bugler to sound boots and saddles. Ten minutes after the attack his whole command thundered out of the camp at Foley into the darkness heading south, for that was the direction he had determined, by lantern light, that the Kid had gone.

They rode at a steady run for fifteen minutes. By then, MacBrayer had calmed down. By then he had admitted to himself that this was foolish and useless. They had no trail. They had no idea where the Kid was headed. They were simply wearing out their horses on a wild-goose chase.

He called a halt. He gave the men and their horses half an hour to rest and then headed dejectedly back to Foley.

They rode to the railroad station at a dragging walk. The horses had been cooled by having their saddles removed, by being rubbed down with coarse saddle blankets. They did not reach Foley until first light was showing on the horizon.

MacBrayer ordered his sergeant to disband the troops. He himself went to his tent, got a bottle out of his duffel bag and took a drink. He followed that with another and with another still.

The three drinks had no effect on him. He thought of the men he would have to bury today and he thought of the five letters he would have to write. He thought of the report he would have to make to his superiors.

They had not expected him to catch the Apache Kid. They had known that was impossible. But they'd not expected him to let himself be attacked, to lose five men to a single Apache because he'd had no sentries out.

Yet at the same time he realized that having sentries out wouldn't have made any difference. The Apache Kid could enter a camp full of snoring men in the middle of the night as easily as a fox can enter a henhouse, only being discovered when he attacked.

He could rationalize that way. But he couldn't completely convince himself. He was still filled with guilt when Frank Healy and Nogal rode into his camp at sunup.

They came immediately to his tent. Frank Healy had seen the five bodies wrapped in burial shrouds over which some men were rigging a sun shelter out of canvas to protect them from the sun until it was time for the funeral. MacBrayer said sourly, 'Don't ask. We've been scouring this goddam desert ever since you left, without turning up a track. I didn't put out sentries last night and that sonofabitch slit the throats of five of my men before somebody woke up and discovered him.'

Healy looked at the man and saw the pain in his eyes, the guilt and self-blame in his face. He asked, 'Did he get any horses?'

'Two. Left his own two worn-out nags.'

'Alive?' Healy was surprised.

MacBrayer nodded. 'Maybe he didn't have time to slit their throats. By that time, all my men were up.'

Healy nodded. Nogal was already questing around looking for a trail but it had been pounded into the earth by MacBrayer's men last night. Healy said, 'Good luck, Lieutenant,' and walked away.

MacBrayer called after him, 'Do you need anything? Provisions? Horses?'

Healy shook his head. Unlike the Apache Kid, both he and Nogal had three horses each. Two of Nogal's were always traveling without any weight. One of Healy's was.

He found Nogal at the edge of the bivouac, looking angry. He said, 'Let's follow it out. They didn't have any light so they must have missed it someplace.'

Glumly and without speaking, Nogal took up the trail of MacBrayer's men. He followed the broad, deeply indented trail for almost a mile before it veered unexpectedly to the right and Nogal picked up the trail of the Apache Kid. The prints were those of big cavalry remounts but there were only two of them and both men knew they had to have been made by the Apache Kid and his prisoner.

From there on, it was a matter of trying to sort out the tracks of their quarry from those of the pursuing cavalrymen. Eventually however they came to the place where the cavalry had abandoned the chase and turned back, and after that it was easy. Nogal led, his eyes on the ground, his horse held at a pace that equaled the pace set by the Apache Kid. The trial went south, and after a while Nogal turned his head and looked at Frank.

'Looks like we've worn him down. He's headed for the Sierra Madre.'

'Then he'll have to get rid of those cavalry horses.'

'He'll attack a Mexican village and steal some burros.'

Healy felt depressed. The Sierra Madre towered nearly twice as high from the desert floor as the Rocky Mountains did from the plain out of which they rose. They were steeper and, unlike the Rockies, were covered with vegetation through which it was sometimes impossible to penetrate.

Water was scarce in spite of the fact that rains sometimes drenched the land for days.

Game was plentiful, but killing that game was nearly impossible due to the heavy growth of vegetation that covered everything.

Not for nothing had Victorio made those mountains a refuge from his enemies. They had been used by Cochise, too, and by every other Apache leader, harried to the point where he had to have a place where he could rest, safe from his enemies.

When they needed supplies, they could come down out of the mountains and raid the small Mexican towns and settlements. They could get burros, food, sometimes women and children if they wanted them.

Healy understood now why the Kid had attacked MacBrayer's camp last night. He had wanted to be followed. He had wanted the trooper's big cavalry horses to wipe out the trail he made. He had known that doing so would gain him at least an hour today, and it had. But he must have counted on more delay than he'd gotten because Healy and Nogal were now very close to him. The hoofprints of the two horses the Kid had stolen were sharp and clear.

They were traveling at either a lope or a run, which told Healy the Kid had a particular Mexican village in mind where he would abandon them and obtain either burros or short-legged ponies for the torturous climb into the mountains.

Neither Healy nor Nogal knew it when they crossed the Mexican border. But they knew they were in Mexico when they saw a detachment of Mexican Rurales approaching on a course that would intersect with theirs.

Healy cursed. He needed neither the delay nor the argument he knew was going to ensue. It was a damn good thing Nogal spoke a little Spanish because his was limited to half a dozen words.

They pulled up when the Mexican troops halted directly in front of them. The commanding officer was a lieutenant, dark and obviously with much Indian blood. He wore a bushy mustache and was stocky and strong across the shoulders and through the chest.

He rattled off a barrage of Spanish, directly at Healy, who spread his hands helplessly and said, '*No hablo*.'

The Mexican looked at Nogal, his eyes hard because Nogal was Apache. Healy noticed that every one of the troopers' muskets was pointed either at him or at Nogal.

He said, 'Tell them we are following the Apache Kid, who has stolen my wife and killed many gringos and many Mexicans.'

Nogal spoke Spanish rapidly to the lieutenant. Obviously the lieutenant understood although he frowned with concentration and Healy guessed that Nogal's Spanish was not as flawless as it could have been.

He spoke to Nogal and when he had finished, Nogal turned to Healy. 'He says we have to go with him, that we are trespassing on Mexican soil.'

'Did you tell him about the Apache Kid?'

Nogal nodded. 'It made no difference.'

'Tell him you will show him the trail of the Apache Kid. But don't make any sudden moves. Those damned muskets may be single-shot, but every one of them is pointed straight at us.'

Nogal spoke to the lieutenant. Healy heard him say, '*Con permiso*,' and then he dismounted and walked through the troopers to where he could point out the trail.

The lieutenant spoke to Nogal again as he returned to and remounted his horse. Nogal said, 'He says we will have to go with him or go back. He says he and his men will follow the trail. They will kill the Kid and rescue your wife and return her to you.'

Healy uttered a muffled obscenity. In the first place, the Rurales had no more chance than a snowball in hell of ever catching up with the Kid. In the second place, even if they did catch up, they would only ensure Nora's death.

Healy considered the alternatives for a moment or so. He would not go back and if he let himself be taken to wherever this lieutenant's headquarters were, he and Nogal might be detained until the commanding officer asked for instructions as to what he should do and that might take weeks.

On the other hand, trying to escape was out

of the question. There were a dozen troopers with the lieutenant, all with muskets pointed straight at them. To Nogal he said, 'Tell him we'll go with him and talk to his commanding officer.'

Nogal spoke to the lieutenant in Spanish. The man seemed satisfied, although a glint of suspicion remained in his dark eyes. He didn't trust Nogal because he was an Apache, and he didn't trust any gringo. On the other hand, he couldn't see how anything could go wrong. If he put half his troops ahead of his prisoners, half behind, they'd have a hard time escaping.

Healy rode ahead of Nogal, but Nogal kept his horse close enough so that his head touched the hindquarter of Healy's mount. This way they could talk without their talk being too noticeable.

They had to get away. That was obvious to both men. And they had to do it soon because they had left the trail of the Apache Kid and were now traveling on a quadrant that took them ever farther and farther toward the west.

Nogal, ever stingy with his words, said, 'I'll say when. You go right and I go left. Keep whatever cover there is between you and them and leave behind all the horses but the one you're on.'

Healy nodded to show he'd understood. The lieutenant turned his head and shouted at Nogal.

They traveled another half mile, finally

entering a little draw where the trail wound among a thick clump of mesquite bushes each of which was higher than their heads.

Just as Healy was about to enter the thicket, Nogal said softly, 'Now,' and immediately afterward turned in his saddle and uttered a shriek that must have been some kind of Apache war cry. The horses of the Mexican troopers immediately behind them, plodding along placidly, were so startled by the sudden shriek that some of them reared, dumping their equally placid riders into the dust. The others whirled and bolted.

Those ahead of Healy and Nogal bolted straight ahead. But neither Healy nor Nogal saw them emerge from the thicket. Nogal had spurred his mount to the left. Healy lashed his horse's rump with the ends of the reins and thanked God the Mexican lieutenant had not disarmed either Nogal or him.

There were shouts and shots behind, and a half-hearted pursuit, with the lieutenant's force divided into three segments, one that pursued Healy, another that pursued Nogal and a third that remained where they were, with the lieutenant in charge.

Healy galloped hard over the uneven ground, taking advantage of every pile of rocks, every clump of brush, until he was out of the range of the Mexicans' old smoothbore muskets. Then he slowed, not enough to let the pursuit catch up, but enough to watch the ground in hopes of picking up the Apache Kid's trail again.

Gradually the Rurales fell behind. They were taking almost as much time firing and then reloading their muskets as they were trying to catch up with him. He was able to put his full attention on the ground, while holding the horse to a trot. He didn't worry about Nogal. He knew the Apache would find him no matter where he went.

He had traveled nearly two miles before he saw the hoofprints of two horses on the ground. To be sure, he dismounted and knelt. These were the Kid's horses, all right. Both were shod. Both had the long-legged gait that is so characteristic of cavalry remounts. As usual, the Kid was holding them to a lope.

Healy kicked his own horse into a lope. Glancing behind, he saw that the Rurales were still a quarter mile behind and with his own horse at a lope, were falling quickly farther and farther behind.

He traveled for another several miles before he saw a lone horseman closing with him on the left. Nogal. Nogal came abreast, grinning as widely as the Apache ever grinned. Healy asked, 'You all right?'

Nogal nodded.

Healy asked, 'How long before they'll give up?'

'An hour.' He dismounted, knelt and carefully studied the trail left by Nora's horse and the Kid's. When he straightened he said, 'Two hours ahead. Maybe three.'

He had scarcely finished speaking when they crested a low ridge and saw before them a small Mexican settlement. The church was the largest building in town. The people were crowding into its doors.

One, a man, turned and saw Healy and Nogal. Immediately he shouted a warning. The people crowded on into the church doors with even more alacrity, fearful now. Two of the men remained outside and, raising old single-shot rifles, fired at Healy and Nogal.

Healy said, 'He's been here.'

The two men in front of the church, apparently unable to reload their guns, had disappeared inside and barred the heavy doors.

Healy stopped. He said, 'They'll stay put until we leave. Cast around and see what the Kid did with his horses and whether he left here on burros.'

Nogal departed immediately. Healy realized suddenly how he must look to these simple Mexicans. He hadn't shaved for three weeks. He hadn't bathed or changed his clothes for at least that long. He must look as savage and dangerous to these villagers as any Apache ever did.

He followed Nogal. The two cavalry horses lay with their throats cut in front of a tiny corral made of cactus and mesquite. Inside were several burros and one horse, a swaybacked ancient that looked at them out of bleary eyes.

They didn't have much choice. But Healy had an idea that might put them closer to the Kid. He said, 'Let's keep these horses and lead two burros each. The horses will make the burros run and we might close up a little before we wear them out.'

Nogal nodded. They caught four burros out of the corral. Healy shouted toward the church and waved some money in the air. Then he placed it on the ground and put a rock over it.

Then they were on their way. Nogal quickly found the trail. They followed it at a fast trot, with the burros loping, pulling back on their halter ropes, behind.

CHAPTER EIGHTEEN

Healy and Nogal continued to ride their horses until they reached the foot of the mountains, about fifteen miles from the Mexican village where they'd gotten the burros. By now, in the day's heavy heat, both horses and burros were sweating, and the burros were threatening to break their halter ropes, so determinedly did they resist being pulled along.

Nogal and Healy stopped. They released the two horses not knowing whether they'd ever find their way back or not. They cached their saddles and whatever other gear they would be unable to take on the burros. With only bridles and saddle blankets and with the two burros they were leading carrying their blanket rolls and saddlebags, they mounted the little animals and followed the Kid's trail upward through cedar and piñon pine, vegetation that quickly changed to jack pine and later to tall, stately pines with needles three or four inches long.

The trail was exceedingly steep and even the Kid had halted often to rest his burros because he knew that if he killed them no more were going to be available.

Healy and Nogal followed his example, resting their burros often. The little animals cooled eventually from the fifteen-mile run they'd had from the village to the foot of the mountains, and now they plodded upward, at their own pace, unhurried and unhurriable.

Once, Healy looked back at his Apache friend. Many times he had wanted to express sympathy for the savage murder of Nogal's wife and boy but he knew Apaches well enough to know the words were better left unsaid. He asked, 'Know where he's going?'

Nogal nodded. 'I know.'

'How far?'

'Forty, fifty miles.'

'Top of the Sierra?'

'Yes. The land is nearly level there. There is much grass and great, tall trees. There is water and all the game a man could want. My people have always gone to that place when they were hard pressed by their enemies.'

Healy knew the only effective enemy the Apaches had ever had had been the United States Army. Other tribes feared them and avoided them when possible and so did the Mexican cavalry.

All day they climbed, resting the burros often, but trying to maintain a pace equal to that of the Apache Kid. In late afternoon great, tall, puffy thunderheads began appearing ahead of them. Healy knew it was going to rain and knew as well that the Kid's trail would be washed out. But Nogal showed no concern, even after the first huge drops began to fall. He knew where to find the Apache Kid.

Lightning slashed down, striking trees and setting them ablaze, but the rain came so soon afterward and so heavily, that the lightning-started fires were extinguished almost as rapidly as they had been kindled.

Deer, having taken shelter in the thick grove of trees, bounded out ahead of them, stiff-legged yet graceful and beautiful. A herd of javelinas, at a higher altitude Healy thought than they usually were, crashed through the brush, getting away.

Nogal finally pulled up beneath a tall and spreading pine, taking a position that would ensure protection from the rain. Healy joined him. No trail was left and there would be none farther on unless Nora managed to leave scraps of cloth along the way. Even that wouldn't be likely to do any good. If they happened to be a quarter mile to one side or the other, they'd never see them anyway.

But Frank Healy knew the chase was drawing to a close. From the crest of the Sierra Madre, there was no place else the Apache Kid could go. It was there, on that level, beautifully forested land, that this grisly business would be played out. He prayed more fervently than he ever had in his life—that Nora would still be alive and unmaimed when he and Nogal arrived. But he knew the chances weren't very good.

* * *

There was no saddle on the burro Nora was given to ride and on the steep trail she slid off the chunky animal's rump three times before she learned that the way to avoid it was to encircle the animal's neck with her arms and grip his belly tightly with her legs.

The Kid seemed to be having no trouble at all. He rode the burro as he rode a horse, as if he was a part of it, no more easily dislodged than any other part of the burro's body.

The trail climbed steeply and steadily. Cedars and piñon pine gave way to stunted jack pine and then to the tall, red-trunked pines.

Water cascaded down gullies and in places made waterfalls as much as twenty or thirty feet high. There were strange plants she had never seen before, and flowers whose beauty surpassed anything she had ever seen.

Yet her joy in the beauty of the place was tempered by her knowledge that the chase was close to its end. She knew about the Apache refuge in the Sierra Madre, where Cochise had taken his followers, and Victorio, and even Geronimo with his ragtag, exhausted little band of cold-blooded murderers.

When she saw the heavy thunderclouds and the savage strikes of lightning, she knew the trail was going to be washed out, and furtively she began tearing small pieces of cloth from her petticoat. Almost as soon as she had started, however, she realized how futile the gesture was. If Nogal and Frank were even a few hundred yards to right or left of the trail she and the Kid were leaving, they would miss the scraps of cloth. And if she was caught dropping them by the Apache Kid, reprisal would be swift.

The rain came, at first in great drops that, when they hit a rock, wet an area nearly two inches in diameter. Then came a burst of sleet, and after that a thunderous, incredibly heavy rain that almost instantly filled every gully with rushing, muddy water, whose sound obscured all other sounds, even that of the howling wind and the falling deluge. Great rocks tumbled down the gullies carried by the rushing water. The sound of the rocks crashing against each other beneath the muddy water was like no sound Nora had ever heard before.

The Kid found shelter beneath a towering pine, whose upper half was bent fiercely by the wind.

Nora slid off her burro and collapsed to the ground. She felt weaker than she ever had before. She felt as if she wanted to die right here so that she wouldn't have to get up and go on.

The Kid paid no attention to her. He rested on the thick carpet of needles beneath the huge tree.

Nora's weakness angered her and yet she knew its cause. She'd had little to eat since she'd been kidnapped. They'd been on the move almost constantly and when she was allowed to sleep it was usually for no more than five or six hours. But, she told herself, the Kid must also be tired, except that he was tougher to begin with and better able to stand the constant movement, poor food and lack of sleep.

She closed her eyes and the world seemed to whirl. Sleep came quickly, but it was not an easy sleep. She dreamed, uneasy dreams that had their roots in her childhood. She had been raised among boys mostly, having preferred their company to that of girls. She had fought with them, played ball with them, shot marbles on the parade and she'd always pretty much held up her end. She wasn't afraid of any boy on the post, a fact she often proved with her fists and knees and feet, and her vocabulary included every cussword known and used by either men or boys on the post. When she was angry she screeched them out and her father despaired of ever making a lady out of her.

And then Frank Healy came to the fort and signed on as a scout. From the first time she saw him, she knew he was for her. But how would she get him, with dirty face and tangled hair and dust all over her from rolling on the ground fighting with a red-haired, skinny boy four inches taller than herself?

Frank Healy had looked down at her, a grin touching the corners of his mouth. And even while she wanted him and knew she'd do anything she had to to get him, she hated him for that half smile.

She awoke to a particularly loud crack of thunder. A tree less than fifty yards away was afire. Rain killed the fire, but the tree smoked for some time before the rain completely put the fire out.

Turning from a tomboy into a lady had been hard for Nora. She'd felt awkward in dresses, and her hair had been neglected for so long it was hard to manage and had little shine to it.

Girl's shoes felt awkward on her feet. But she persevered, and at last the time came when Frank Healy strode across the dance floor at the fort and asked her for a dance.

She danced awkwardly, furious at herself

because she hadn't taken the time and trouble to get one of the ladies on the post to teach her how to dance. But she was naturally graceful and by the time she'd danced the last three dances with Frank Healy was following him fairly well.

Between that dance and the next, she learned the steps. She worked harder on her appearance. And at the next dance, when Frank Healy came toward her it was not on a whim but purposefully, as if he was drawn to her as much as she was drawn to him.

Their actual courtship was brief, broken only by a couple of ineffectual campaigns against the Indians. And when at last he asked Mike Corcoran for her hand, she hid, shivering with delight, in the bedroom, waiting for her father to give his consent.

Which he did, without hesitation. For one thing, he was glad to be rid of her and of the worry she caused him. It wasn't that he didn't love her. But she worried him. He saw what a beauty she was becoming, and he was afraid.

But he admired Frank, despite the fact that Frank was older than she. And he approved of him as a son-in-law, particularly after he learned that Frank had no intention of continuing as a scout and intended, instead, to seek out a good piece of rangeland and raise cattle and kids on it.

The cattle had not been difficult. The kids had. Not until recently had Nora been able to conceive. And now she was as deathly afraid of miscarrying as she was of being killed by the Apache Kid. The first few months of a pregnancy were, she knew, the crucial ones. By her docility, she had managed to avoid a savage beating at the hands of the Apache Kid. But she had a feeling that he had terrible plans for her once they reached the safety of the Apache mountain refuge. He wanted more than Healy's, her and Nogal's deaths. He wanted them to suffer, if possible to make them scream out with pain. And if he could never make Healy scream with pain, at least he could make him scream inwardly when he viewed the awful things he would have done to her.

The rain lasted for nearly three hours. When it was over, leaving brush and trees dripping, the Kid signaled her curtly to mount, and the two little burros, more sure-footed than horses could ever be, resumed the climb.

They camped that night in a small clearing that still was soaked by the day's heavy rain. As usual, the Kid set up a dummy camp in the center of the clearing, then, with Nora, retreated into the thick brush and timber that surrounded it.

He cooked no fire, and she ate as much of the raw meat he gave her as she could. It was beginning to smell and it took every bit of her will power to force it down.

Afterward, the Kid tied her hands and feet again with the leather thongs. He disappeared into the darkness and moments after he had gone, the woods were silent, except for the occasional movement of the burros in the clearing, or the drip of water from the trees.

She didn't know whether he had settled down to sleep or whether he was doing something deadlier, like working his way back along the trail to the place, which could not be far, where Frank and Nogal had camped.

She cried out, simulating a cry of pain, but received no response. That he had not responded did not mean the Kid had gone. But she was terribly afraid he had.

She prayed, more desperately than ever before, that Frank and Nogal were on guard. If they were not, one or both of them would die.

CHAPTER NINETEEN

Frank Healy and Nogal camped about five miles behind the Kid and Nora, choosing, as the Kid had, a huge spreading pine to shelter them. Underneath, where the carpet of pine needles was several inches thick, the ground was dry.

They ate dry rations, of which they had a considerable variety compared to the Kid's raw horse meat. Nogal volunteered to watch for the first half of the night, while Healy slept. He was to call Healy at midnight to take over the watch. Both men knew they were close to the Apache Kid. Both knew how unpredictable he was and suspected that before the night was over he might attack their camp.

Frank Healy lay down, hollowed out a place in the blanket of pine needles for his shoulder, and another for his hip. The chill of night came down, cold enough simply from the altitude but colder because of the rain. He pulled his blanket over him, looked at Nogal's dark shape where he sat on a nearby rock, and closed his eyes.

But he couldn't sleep. Nora must be near exhaustion, he thought. He was himself, and he was a lot tougher and used to hardship than she. Right now she was somewhere up ahead, probably tied hand and foot and gagged beneath just such a pine as the one which towered over him. And the Kid . . . well, one thing was almost certain. He wouldn't be sleeping. What would he be doing? And then Frank knew this was the night the Kid had waited for. He was probably now retracing his steps back along the trail he had made today, searching for his pursuers.

He knew he would not find them on his trail. That had been washed away. But he'd find them. Either his burro would smell theirs and give away their location or vice versa. He'd locate them and after that would move in as silent as any stalking cat until he was close enough to strike.

Healy got up, folded his blanket and laid it on a rock. He walked silently to Nogal and said, 'This is the night. He's coming. I can't sleep, knowing that, and I don't think you can either.'

Nogal grunted agreement. Had Nogal been another white man, it was possible Healy would have sat down nearby, with his back to the other, just to feel the closeness and companionship. But he knew Nogal would not approve of this. If the Apache Kid was coming, they should be separated by at least fifty yards. So that the Kid must attack each one separately. So that he couldn't make his attack against both simultaneously.

The night was almost utterly still, the only sound being the drip of water from the pines and the still-running, but diminishing rush of water in the gullies and ravines. Overhead, the clouds had passed away and the sky was clear, filled with its millions upon millions of stars and the blue that was the Milky Way.

There was no longer any wind. Not a leaf stirred. But occasionally one of the burros shifted his feet or changed position, and whenever that happened, both Nogal and Healy turned their heads toward the sound.

It had been a hard day, a long day, like so many that had gone before. Healy began to feel drowsy and his eyelids drooped. Angrily he shook his head. One thing neither of them could afford tonight was drowsiness. Tonight it was kill or be killed. Tonight he might be able, after the Kid was dead, to trail him back to where he had left Nora tied. He might, at last, rescue his wife.

The thought lifted his spirits and drove all drowsiness away. He let himself anticipate holding her in his arms again. She would be weak. She would have lost a great deal of weight. But here, in this place, they could rest until her strength returned. They could then make their way back at a leisurely pace. Eventually they could return to their ranch and take up life at the point the Apache Kid had so cruelly interrupted it.

He couldn't understand the feeling of depression that gradually crept over him. Was it possible that, before leaving his camp tonight, the Kid had murdered Nora, mutilated her and left her for him to find in the morning?

Yes, he thought, it was possible. With the Kid, anything was possible. But if he had done that, the Kid would not attack Frank Healy if and when he found their camp. He would go after Nogal, wanting to leave Healy alive.

He fixed his glance on Nogal and kept it there, relying on his hearing to reveal the Kid's presence when he came. He listened intently, knowing how stealthy the Kid could be, knowing too that the wet ground made silence even easier for him.

He knew suddenly that Nogal was the only one in danger, and realized with something close to panic that if the Kid attacked Nogal there would be no time for him to reach the pair. No time to save Nogal's life if he was genuinely surprised.

He got up and started toward Nogal, and at the same time saw a darker shadow closing with Nogal from the rear. He roared, 'Nogal! Behind you!'

He was running now, as fast as he had ever run in his life before. He couldn't shoot, because by now the two dark shapes had joined. He snatched the skinning knife from its scabbard on his belt.

At that instant, he either tripped on a rock or root, or slipped on the wet pine needles underfoot. He sprawled forward, both arms extended to halt his fall and push him to his feet again as quickly as possible.

He made it to his feet, having taken his eyes off the struggling pair only briefly. They were still locked in combat, but even as he watched one broke away. Bent over, nearly double, he ran from the scene.

Nogal was writhing on the ground, and Healy hesitated for the briefest instant between pursuing the fleeing Apache Kid, who obviously was wounded, or going to his friend and rendering assistance now when it would count the most. By the time he had considered the choice, however briefly, it was too late to go after the Apache Kid, and maybe too late for Nogal as well.

He knelt at Nogal's side, not touching him,

trying to tell from the scout's movements where he was hurt. Nogal whispered, 'I got him. I got him in the gut.'

'Where did he get you? That's the important thing.'

'Chest. I'm finished. You go after him. He's hurt bad, he'll kill your wife as soon as he gets back to camp.'

Healy knew that was true. But he couldn't leave Nogal. Decency wouldn't permit it no matter how worried he was about his wife. He said, 'Wait a minute. I'll find some dry cloth to stop the blood.'

He got up and went to his saddlebags. He had a clean shirt in one of them although only God knew why he was carrying a clean shirt on this bloody, dirty chase. He pulled it out and turned.

He saw the flash just an instant before he heard the roar of the report. He didn't have to kneel at Nogal's side to know what the scout had done. Aware that if Healy stayed his wife would die, and also aware that his own death was but a matter of minutes or an hour at best, he had taken his own life, quickly and without hesitation, so that Healy could go.

Healy put a hand on Nogal's chest. There was no movement. He straightened up, aware of the blood on his hand. He wiped it on the shirt and threw the shirt away.

Angry now, furiously so, he sprinted for the place the burros had been tied. The Kid would have killed them if he'd had the time and if he'd not been hurt. But he'd had no time, and he was hurt. Nogal had said he'd stabbed him in the gut.

It was a wound that would eventually be fatal unless it was treated by a doctor, which it wouldn't be. But it was also a wound that, except for pain, would scarcely disable a man as fierce and single-minded, with the will power of the Apache Kid. He had left the place where he'd killed Nogal bent over but at a run. Healy was willing to bet he had already straightened up. He might be bleeding internally, but probably not very much. He was strong enough and tough enough to reach his camp, kill Nora and be waiting for Healy when he came.

Healy untied one of the burros. With his knife he cut the halter rope off the other one's halter. It would make a good whip and he was going to need a whip.

The smell of blood on him frightened the burro and when the length of rope came down savagely across his rump, he broke into a trot up the hill. And Healy prayed, 'O God, let me find his camp right away!'

Searching around for it, even for a few minutes, meant the difference between failure and success. Even if he found it right away, he knew the Kid was capable of using Nora as a shield, especially wounded as he was. And worse, Healy knew a gunshot might let him know the location of the Kid's camp. The gunshot that killed Nora or crippled her.

Savagely he continued to lash the burro's rump. Surefooted as he was, the little animal slipped and slid on the muddy ground and on the slick pine needles beneath the trees.

At last, realizing he could make as much progress on foot, Healy slid off the burro and tied him swiftly to a scrubby tree. He went on, lunging upward, sometimes falling, but always going on. In his mind was a picture of Nora, the way she had been when last he saw her, and that picture gave his feet speed they had never had before.

He didn't want to yell, and he assumed Nora had been gagged. But she had not been gagged. Suddenly, from his right he heard a short cry, obviously hers.

He swerved at top speed, heading toward the sound. There was cold horror in his mind because he well knew that might have been Nora's last cry. He tried to urge even more speed from his straining body, while being very careful that nothing tripped him, that his feet did not go out from under him. Loss of footing had cost Nogal's life, or might have. It mustn't be allowed to happen now.

He heard the cry again, this time less than a dozen yards away. And suddenly he stopped.

Going straight to Nora would be the equivalent of committing suicide. The Kid was waiting, and would close with him as he knelt at Nora's side.

He took a stance beside the rough trunk of a towering pine. He strained his eyes into the darkness. In the nearly complete stillness, he could hear her whisper, 'Frank, be careful. He's here, and he'll kill you if he can.'

Her soft voice made his chest ache for fear for her. That whispered warning might be her death warrant. But he had her spotted now, a dark shape against the lighter sky beyond this ridge.

If the Kid closed in to kill her, he would be too late. But the Kid was hurt. And he didn't think simply killing Nora was going to satisfy him.

He wanted Healy helpless and hurt and unable to intervene. And then, with Healy watching, he wanted to torture Nora until she was screaming her pain into the night.

In this perverted desire on the Kid's part to inflict pain lay Healy's only chance. He wanted to reassure Nora but he didn't dare give his position away. He stood there, rifle in one hand, knife in the other, pressing himself against the rough trunk of the giant pine. His ears heard each small sound and his eyes caught every movement, even the stir of a pine branch ten feet overhead.

The chase had reached its end. The next five minutes would decide who lived and who died. Or worse, whether Nora spent the rest of her life a helpless cripple, her beauty and mobility destroyed to satisfy the perverted thirst for vengeance in the Apache Kid.

CHAPTER TWENTY

The Apache Kid returned to his camp about five minutes ahead of Frank. He knew he was seriously wounded and that he would probably never leave this place alive. But he had to know how long he had before the wound incapacitated him.

He went to Nora immediately. She was tied but not gagged and was no threat to him. He bared his belly and showed her the wound in the light of a sulphur match. He asked, 'How long I got?'

She couldn't tell for sure. She wasn't a doctor. The wound was low on his abdomen, a narrow bluish hole from which little blood had come. The bleeding was inside, and might be heavy or light, depending on what arteries or veins the bullet had cut as it went on through. Furthermore, how active the Kid was in the next half hour had a bearing on how long he lived. The more active he was, the more he would bleed internally.

It was even possible that he wouldn't die at all. If he remained quiet for a week or two, he might recover from the wound. She said, 'It doesn't look very serious. I don't even think you're going to die. Not from that wound, at least.'

He grunted, pulled down his shirt and got to his feet. He listened intently, then on silent feet disappeared into the darkness.

Nora couldn't hear anything. But she knew the Kid had heard. Something. Something alien, probably Frank coming up the trail.

She uttered another cry, wordless, that the Kid might think was a cry of pain because of lack of circulation in her arms and legs. She knew it would be enough. It would let Frank know where she was. It would warn him that the Apache Kid was nearby, waiting only for the most advantageous moment to attack.

She heard nothing after that. No sound from the Kid. None from Frank. She lay utterly still, scarcely daring to breathe. Her cry might bring the Kid back, furious, to make her pay for uttering it. But she didn't think so. It would be an unnecessary chance she doubted the Kid would take.

The advantage should be with Frank. At least it should if Nogal was with him. But something inside her told her that Nogal was dead. That the Kid had killed him a while ago when he left camp so silently. Now it was between Frank and the Kid, with the only thing likely to even up the contest being the Apache Kid's belly wound.

But maybe Frank was wounded too, she thought. She lay there still and prayed, and tried to banish all her doubting thoughts. And the darkness around her was as silent as the grave, except for the occasional drip of water from the tree under which she lay. And except for the distant rush of water in some deep ravines, still running off the mountains high above.

She waited, and to herself she whispered, 'Oh, Frank, for God's sake be careful! I love you. We love you. And we want you back alive!'

Would he believe this child was his? Indeed, would he even care? Those were questions that had no answers now. Later she would know. But before she did, a battle to the death must be fought here in the darkness. And there wasn't a single thing she could do to change the outcome of that fight. She could only wait.

Nora's cries had told Healy where the Kid's camp was. They were more than he had expected and, wordless though they had been, he knew Nora had uttered them for the specific purpose of letting him locate her.

Now, if he did what was expected of him, he would head for the sound, where the Kid would be waiting to attack him while he was releasing his wife.

But by now he knew the Kid's devious mind, knew how he thought. Going to Nora was the obvious thing, so the Kid would expect almost anything else.

Which made going to her the unexpected. Silently, a careful step at a time, he headed for the place from which Nora's cries had come, only shifting his knife to the right hand, his rifle to the left. The Kid wouldn't be far from Nora but perhaps, if he was silent enough, he could reach her and release her before the Kid attacked him like a hawk swooping down on a prairie dog.

The next few minutes seemed like hours to him. Healy could see her, hardly distinguishable from a large rock or bush. He could hear her breathing and see an occasional movement she made to improve the circulation in her arms or legs.

He searched the surrounding area for any darker shape that might be the Kid. Seeing none, he came in with a rush, laying aside his rifle and immediately putting his hand over her mouth.

By feel, he located the thongs on her wrists and ankles and slashed them with his knife. Then, without even speaking in a whisper to her, giving her no instructions because he knew she needed none, he got to his feet and started away.

A body struck him, knocking him from his feet but not before his hand had recovered the rifle from the ground. Like a hot iron the Kid's knife slashed across the muscles of his back, bringing instant pain and an instant rush of blood.

He let himself fall to the ground, and then rolled, and held the Kid's second attack off with his rifle, held in both his hands. He had dropped his knife and knew he could not recover it.

The Kid slashed again, savagely, with his knife. Its razor-sharp blade slid along the barrel of the rifle, coming to a stop when it struck the receiver, and then Healy had forced the Apache away and was swinging the gun, bringing it to bear.

But the Kid was already disappearing into the night. Healy fired at his dark, dim shape, but he didn't know whether his bullet had struck home or not. The Kid was gone.

So was Nora. During the scuffle she had done what she knew Frank would want her to. She had fled, as silently as she could, so that he would not have her to worry about while he fought the Kid.

At last, thought Frank, it had come down to the essentials he had hoped for so long. Nora was out of it, or should be. The Kid was wounded at least as seriously as he. Healy was bleeding profusely from the knife slash, which was at least a quarter inch deep. In places the knife had been stopped only by the bone.

He crouched there silently, listening, at a disadvantage because the Kid knew exactly where he was while he had not the faintest notion where the Kid had gone.

Cautiously he eased himself to his feet. He held the rifle in both hands now, ready to use it either as a club, a shield, or to fire it. Carefully and silently, he moved away, heading toward the huge tree trunk that had sheltered him before.

There was a sound, a rush of wind and at the last the movement of a rock nearby. The Kid struck him again, but this time Healy had enough warning to raise his rifle and fend him off. But the extended knife got through and slashed the muscles of his forearm, bringing a second rush of blood. He thought, 'God, I'm going to have to do better or he's going to cut me to bits.' He brought the gun to bear a second time and fired and this time was rewarded by seeing the Kid's dark shape disappear as he sprawled on the ground.

Healy didn't hesitate. He plunged forward, rifle ready as he jacked a fresh cartridge into it. But the dark shape of the Kid was on the ground only an instant. Then it was up, and running, and again Healy headed for the tree trunk to wait. He hoped Nora had put enough distance between the two of them and herself so that she would be safe. His heart sank and his chest turned cold when he heard her cry, not a hundred yards up the hill, where the Kid had apparently accidentally intercepted her and made her prisoner again.

No longer could Healy afford to wait. The Kid was hurt, twice, and as dangerous as a teased rattlesnake. He pushed himself away from the tree and plunged recklessly up the hill toward the sound of Nora's voice. He cursed himself silently. He should have determined which way she had gone and put himself between her and the Kid. But he had not, and now he had to reach her before the Kid did her any harm.

The darkness was almost absolute, but fortunately the ground underfoot was level or nearly so and relatively free of stumps and roots and rocks. Healy traveled at a dead run, with no time to watch the ground, searching frantically ahead for the two dark shapes or the blended single one that would be Nora and the Kid.

In his heart he knew he probably had failed. After all these weeks, after all the suffering Nora had endured. Now she was in the hands of the Apache Kid, and before he threw her from him, she would be badly, perhaps mortally hurt.

There was only one way Healy knew to deal with what seemed such an impossible situation. Not with craft. Not with any concern for his own life or safety. He hit the two of them with the full force of his body without even knowing where the blade of the Kid's knife was.

All three sprawled out on the ground, which was rocky here. Healy, having no trouble even in the darkness identifying the Kid, slammed his rifle, still held in both hands, square into the Kid's face.

But he felt the bite of the Kid's knife as he did, raking across the back of a hand, instantly numbing it. He had to kill the Kid and quickly or he'd be killed himself.

Pushing himself away, he shoved the muzzle against the Kid and pulled the trigger, even as the Kid tried desperately and with the litheness of a bobcat to twist himself away. His feet came out, kicking at Healy, and his hands gripped the rifle barrel in a desperate attempt to force it to one side.

Fortunately it had been Healy's left hand he had slashed. His right, on the trigger, squeezed.

The report was muffled by the Kid's body, but even this was not a mortal shot, because the Kid had succeeded in forcing the muzzle partly to the side. The bullet entered his groin.

Healy jacked another cartridge in. The Kid was gone, half lunging, half crawling, and Healy was on his feet instantly in pursuit. But it was like chasing a wounded mountain lion. Sooner or later the Kid would stop. And make his last stand. And show Healy his teeth again.

Recklessly Healy plunged through the night, unthinking that the Kid might turn on him, wanting only, now, to have this over with once and for all.

Behind him, he heard Nora coming, and thanked God she wasn't hurt, at least not seriously. He heard her scream, and at the same time saw the Apache Kid stop, and turn, and with the last of his strength raise up and make a wide slash with his knife.

Healy had to skid to a halt and arch his body

to avoid it. He fired, then, and saw the Kid driven back by the heavy slug which Healy believed had struck him in the chest and hit a bone. He jacked another cartridge in and stood there over the Kid, muzzle pointing down, ready to fire at the slightest movement from the Indian.

But there was none. Healy shoved the rifle muzzle against the Kid's head and fired and only then did he dare turn back to his wife.

She was trembling from head to foot, violently as if she had an awful chill and this was as near hysteria as she would ever get. Her arms went around him and almost immediately came away as she said in a quavering voice. 'You're hurt! Oh God, you're hurt.'

They built a fire, and by its light, Nora bandaged his back with ragged pieces of her petticoat and dress and likewise bandaged his hand. Healy dragged the body of the Kid to the fire, still wanting to be sure this savage killer was really dead.

The sky turned gray with dawn. But neither Nora nor Frank had slept last night. They found a pretty, hidden, place and there they slept, in each other's arms.

At sundown, while Nora still slept wih exhaustion, Frank Healy got up. He covered the Kid's surprisingly slight body with rocks and when Nora awoke, returned and did the same for Nogal. Then, traveling at a leisurely pace, they began their journey down the steep slopes of the Sierra Madre toward their ranch in western New Mexico.

Nora told Frank about their child. She saw the gladness in his eyes and wondered why she had ever worried about what his reaction was going to be.

We hope you have enjoyed this Large Print book. Other Chivers Press or G.K. Hall & Co. Large Print books are available at your library or directly from the publishers.

For more information about current and forthcoming titles, please call or write, without obligation, to:

Chivers Press Limited
Windsor Bridge Road
Bath BA2 3AX
England
Tel. (01225) 335336

OR

G.K. Hall & Co.
P.O. Box 159
Thorndike, Maine 04986
USA
Tel. (800) 223-2336

All our Large Print titles are designed for easy reading, and all our books are made to last.